"What do you want?"

It was *him* again.
show up, yet he'd

"I want to know
uttering the word

"I desire you to leave me alone."

"You're lying. If not to me, then to yourself.
Did you lie to your husband?"

"I don't have a husband. I left him because he
didn't love me enough. His career became his
mistress."

"I wouldn't make that mistake," he assured her
as he lifted her hand to his lips and raked his
teeth back and forth across her knuckles.

Her earlobes began to tingle. She could barely
breathe. "We're total strangers," she said with a
gasp. "You don't have the slightest idea about
what I want."

"With strangers there are no inhibitions....
You've thought about me...wondered what it
would be like if I lost control...lost myself in
you."

"What do you want?" she asked again.

"I want you to be my mistress...."

Dear Reader,

Provocative, evocative and daring – as usual,
Tiffany White has written a story that takes
romance into new realms. In *Forbidden Fantasy*,
a woman explores the dangerous limits of her
wildest fantasies with a mystery lover.

The story is wonderfully shocking but shockingly
wonderful. We would love to hear your reactions
to this special book and encourage you to write to
us, or to fill in the questionnaire which appears at
the end of the book.

The Editor
Mills & Boon Temptation
Eton House
18-24 Paradise Road
Richmond
Surrey
TW9 1SR

Forbidden Fantasy

TIFFANY WHITE

MILLS & BOON LIMITED
ETON HOUSE, 18-24 PARADISE ROAD
RICHMOND, SURREY TW9 1SR

*First published in Great Britain in 1992
by Mills & Boon Limited, Eton House, 18-24 Paradise Road,
Richmond, Surrey TW9 1SR*

© Anna Eberhardt 1991

ISBN 0 263 77850 9

21 - 9207

Made and printed in Great Britain

Prologue

THE EIFFEL TOWER stood sentinel in the background while the dangerous-looking man continued his surveillance, hidden in the crowd of tourists.

His clothing, bomber jacket, T-shirt and jeans, offered no clues about his origin. Dark hair skimmed his wide shoulders and a stubble of fresh beard shadowed the planes of a stubborn jaw.

His eyes, half-concealed beneath thick lashes, were blue—ice blue. Alaskan-frontier blue and just as bleak as they followed the pretty woman whizzing around on skates on the outdoor roller rink. A quick neon blaze of abandon and then she was far away from him.

He was desperate for her. Stolen glimpses were no longer enough.

Soon, he promised himself.

Soon he would *act*.

1

"WHO IS THAT GUY?"

"What guy?" Zoe asked absently, used to Lauren-Claire's endless fascination with the opposite sex. Lauren-Claire noticed all men. In the months since they'd become friends, then loft mates, Zoe had been awed by Lauren-Claire's passion.

The two women had met in a drawing course at the Museum of Decorative Arts just after Zoe had arrived in Paris six months ago. Having put her failed marriage behind her, Zoe's goal was to find herself; to find what it was *she* really wanted. Clichéd, yes, Zoe admitted, but necessary.

A typical Parisian, Lauren-Claire was a romantic, while Zoe didn't have an ounce of romance left in her soul.

"That guy...the *très* gorgeous one I saw watching you skate the other day. Remember, I told you about him."

"Mmm..." Zoe pulled her attention away from the ornate carousel they were riding to look at the crowd. "And I told you that you have an overactive, ah, imagination."

"I do not. I tell you I just saw him again. And he was watching you."

"Okay, so where is he?"

"Back over there." Lauren-Claire pointed. "Wait, you'll see him once the carousel goes back around."

But when the gaily painted horses went around again the man was gone.

"Well, he *was* there," Lauren-Claire said in exasperation. "Why doesn't he introduce himself? He certainly doesn't look like the shy type to me. He looks like a guy used to getting anything he wants."

"Great. Just my type . . . Neanderthal *erectus*."

"Zo-o-e! I'm being serious. He looked intense—kind of dangerous. Maybe you ought to be concerned."

"I promise I'll keep my eyes open. Now will you please forget about this supposed mystery man? I'm starved. Let's get something to eat."

"Okay, but I get to choose," Lauren-Claire insisted, her dark eyes surveying the crowd as they got off the carousel.

"No, no, no," Zoe protested, her golden-blond hair swirling as she shook her head. "I want French food. I'm not eating at McDonald's again."

"So we'll have *le burger, les fries,* and *le shake.*" Lauren-Claire linked her arm through Zoe's with an affectionate giggle.

Lauren-Claire was ten years younger than Zoe, the baby sister she'd never had. Zoe gave in. Lauren-Claire's love for all things American was an endearing quality and one not widely shared by most of her countrymen.

"You're going to burn out on fast food before you even leave for your holiday in the States next week," Zoe warned when they arrived at McDonald's on the Champs Elysées.

"No way," Lauren-Claire scoffed as they placed their orders.

Once they were seated, Lauren-Claire returned to the subject of her upcoming holiday. Her parents, wealthy vineyard owners, sent all of their children to the States after graduation from university. "You promised to tell me the best place to meet cowboys."

"I can't believe you're really serious about this cowboy business."

"Sure I am. I've been wanting me a cowboy ever since I saw my first Clint Eastwood movie."

Zoe swirled the straw in her shake. "Lauren-Claire, there aren't any gunslingers like Clint Eastwood. The Wild West is a thing of the past, and none of it was like the movies."

"I don't believe you. I think 'y'all' Yankee women just want to keep the cowboys to yourselves," Lauren-Claire said, fluffing her short black curls.

"I give up," Zoe said, rolling her eyes at Lauren-Claire's attempt at a drawl complete with French accent.

"Tell you what," Lauren-Claire wheedled, stealing one of Zoe's fries. "If you tell me where the best cowboys are, I'll tell you, ah—" she snapped her fingers "—where the best ice cream in Paris is," she said in a rush. "Maybe even the best ice cream in all of Europe."

"Texas."

"*Alors*, that was easy."

"You know ice cream is my weakness. Come on, give . . . where?"

"Berthillon . . . 31 rue Saint Louis-en-l'Île, to be precise."

They returned to their loft in an old warehouse, after eating the best raspberry ice cream Zoe had ever tasted and Lauren-Claire pulled her well-worn map of the States from her bag. Kicking off her shoes, she made herself comfortable on the sofa as she studied the map.

The loft was furnished sparsely with family castoffs from Lauren-Claire and a few items from Conran's. Zoe hadn't been prepared for the expense of staying in Paris; her nest egg was shrinking at an alarming rate. Lauren-Claire's offer to share had been a real relief.

"Hey, wait a minute! Texas isn't out West."

"Lauren-Claire, you go looking for Clint Eastwood out West and you'll end up with a Malibu cowboy. Trust me, *chérie*, a Malibu cowboy is not what 'y'all' want."

THE NEXT MORNING the older gentleman in a beret smiled when Zoe handed him the sketch she'd drawn. Nodding his satisfaction, he paid her and added a handsome tip.

"That's a great gimmick you have there. I wish I'd thought of it," Lauren-Claire said.

"Gimmick? I don't know what you're talking about. I have the sight. Sit for me and I'll show you."

"Me?"

"Yeah, come on, it'll be fun."

"Okay." Lauren-Claire posed saucily.

Zoe worked slowly, taking her time with each aspect of the drawing until she was satisfied, before moving on. Her deft strokes captured Lauren-Claire's essence on paper. Passersby smiled when they glanced at her work.

"Aren't you done yet?" Lauren-Claire asked, squirming impatiently. Lauren-Claire specialized in sketching pets who never sat still. As Parisians treasured their pets, she supplemented the allowance from her parents quite handsomely.

"Almost done." Zoe added the finishing touches to the sketch with a smile. It had taken her a while, but now she was used to standing on the cobblestone streets of Montmartre, plying her trade as an artist to make a living. She'd traveled to Paris on a whim, but had grown to love the ambience of the Left Bank, its small, winding streets and cafés. Sometimes in nice weather she and Lauren-Claire would sit on the steps of Sacré Coeur and people watch.... Well, Lauren-Claire would man watch.

"Okay, I'm finished."

"Finally. I was beginning to feel like a statue. I even saw some pigeons eyeing me speculatively." Jumping up, Lauren-Claire came around to see Zoe's sketch of her.

"Oh, Zoe! It's fantastic!"

Zoe's specialty was sketching people as they would have looked in a past life. She'd drawn Lauren-Claire in a provocative red dress trimmed with feathers—a dance-hall girl who could have stepped out of a saloon during the gold rush days.

"You can't *really* see into the past, can you?" Lauren-Claire asked in a speculative tone.

"I figure there has to be some reason you have this fixation with cowboys," she answered noncommittally.

Lauren-Claire's eyes took on a far away look. "Oh Zoe, wouldn't you have loved to have lived back then?"

"Not on your life," Zoe answered, folding her easel. "And neither would you...there were no McDonald's."

"Zo-o-e..."

The two of them gathered up their art supplies and headed for the metro station. Their car was packed and Lauren-Claire began flirting outrageously with three young men, university students.

Zoe hung on to the strap and smiled, watching her. It hadn't been all that long since she'd been a dreamer like Lauren-Claire. Maybe that was why she enjoyed her company so. Maybe here in Paris she would find herself again. Begin to live again.

She had come to Paris because of its reputation. She'd wanted to sit at an outdoor café while idling away an afternoon of people watching, ride in an open boat on the Seine, have dinner on a café terrace.... She'd wanted to soak up the city's energy and bustle, to enjoy the romance that was Paris.

In Paris the possibilities were endless. She could do whatever she wanted. Her husband wasn't here to object, to make her put his needs first.

It had been foolish of her, Zoe now knew, to marry so young. But no one could have stopped her. She'd been so in love, so anxious to start married life. Her husband had wanted a stay-at-home wife because of his irregular hours as a cop. It was also a part of his cultural background.

She had been happy in the traditional role at first. But then things had started to go wrong. She'd taken off her rose-colored glasses to find herself trapped and lonely.

She might have been able to bear the loneliness of being a policeman's wife, if only he had talked about his job. But he had refused to discuss his work with her. He'd said he wanted to spare her, that she was a part of his life untouched by the grim realities he had to face every day on the street. He had wanted to keep their home a haven.

When he became a detective their married life worsened. He was hardly ever home, staying away for longer and longer stretches of time in his undercover work.

Days would go by without her hearing from him. When he did come home, he was uncommunicative and withdrawn, shutting her out completely. His work overshadowed everything until he became his work.

One day, coming home from a cooking class—one of many classes she'd busied herself with—to an empty home, she had snapped, unable to take another day of the endless waiting.

Unable to continue to live her life on hold.

At that moment she had been forced to admit that their home was little more than a convenient hotel, where her husband stopped off to change clothes, make love and eat. She no longer knew him and he no longer knew her.

They had become complete strangers.

The last time she'd tried to tell him how unhappy she was with the state of their deteriorating marriage, the discussion had escalated into a full-blown argument ending with another of his punishing silences.

The argument had started when she'd introduced the subject of fantasies, telling him that in his long absences undercover she sometimes pretended she had a fantasy lover. Someone who took her down off the pedestal her husband had placed her on and treated her like the passionate woman she was—or suspected she could be.

He hadn't understood what she was trying so desperately to tell him.

Instead of realizing she wanted him to treat her differently, he'd understood her to want another man. That hadn't been the case at all. She'd loved her husband. The fantasy lover of her daydreams resembled him physically, the difference was emotional. The lover she imagined was emotionally open and available to her.

He was a lover who didn't pat her on the head and dismiss her worries about the dangers of his job. He talked to her. He didn't take her for granted. Instead, he paid careful attention to her. This exquisite attention met her needs as well as his. He allowed her to explore the intimate boundaries of her emotions and sensuality without censure, encouraged her, even.

But it was all just a fantasy.

While her husband was a daringly brave cop, she sensed that her needs and the fact that she had needs at all, frightened him.

The lurch of the subway car pulling into their station pulled Zoe back to the present as she followed Lauren-Claire out of the car. A man brushed past behind her; a fleeting but intimate touch. His cologne lingered in her senses, invasive and sexy.

"Zoe," Lauren-Claire said, motioning to gain her attention.

"What?"

"That was him."

"Who?"

"The guy I've been telling you about," Lauren-Claire's voice was impatient. "Did you see?"

Zoe shook her head. Had he been the one who had...? Oh, for heaven's sake, now Lauren-Claire had her imagining things. The metro car had been crowded, that was all.

"Zoe, quick! There he is!" Lauren-Claire pointed.

All Zoe saw when her eyes followed Lauren-Claire's finger was a pair of broad shoulders in a leather jacket, then he was lost in the surge of the crowd.

"Are you sure?" Zoe asked, turning her attention back to Lauren-Claire.

Lauren-Claire nodded. "Why do you suppose he's following you?"

"You're making too much of this. I'm sure its just some bored Frenchman playing at giving an American a thrill."

"I hope your cowboys are as hospitable," Lauren-Claire said with an engaging grin. "I wouldn't want my holiday to be boring."

"I hardly think there's any danger of that," Zoe said, pulling out a wooden slat chair at a sidewalk café. Digging into her bag, she came up with a handful of francs. "I'll order us coffee if you'll get us a copy of *Le Figaro*."

"Maybe we can catch an early movie," Lauren-Claire suggested.

Their coffee had arrived by the time she returned with the newspaper. After careful deliberation they decided on the movie showing at the Gaumont Ambassade on the Champs Elysées.

Zoe kept an eye out, but there was no sign of Lauren-Claire's mystery man.

She was almost disappointed.

And very foolish, she admonished herself as they rose to leave. Her thoughts had been traveling down reckless paths. She wasn't *that* lonely... was she?

Surely it was only that she missed the times with her husband that had been good. The short stretches of time they'd spent together had been when she'd really lived. But even so, she'd always sensed he was holding back. He had been a sweet and gentle lover, but he had treated her as if she might break.

His abandonment had broken her heart.

And now she had to learn to live without him.

She had to learn to live for herself.

ZOE WANTED to pinch herself to see if she was dreaming. A year ago she would never have imagined her classes would have led to this!

She was at the famed Cordon Bleu cooking school in Paris. The school had only recently begun offering daily cooking demonstrations to visitors. As soon as she had read about it in *Le Figaro*, she had set aside an afternoon to treat herself.

A chef was demonstrating how to make *boeuf bourguignon*. For the tourists his French was translated into English. From her seat, Zoe watched the large mirror over the chef's station as he took them through the steps from ingredients to presentation.

There it was again.

Someone was watching her.

She shifted in her seat, resisting the urge to look over her shoulder. She didn't want to miss what the chef was doing. It didn't matter, she realized; she was missing it, anyway. It was hard to concentrate with the hairs on the back of her neck signaling she was being watched.

She had dismissed the same feeling as being nothing more than her overactive imagination when she'd watched another chef prepare *la terrine de canard au foie gras*. But now she was certain she was being watched.

Surely it wasn't *him*.

No, she was letting Lauren-Claire's fanciful notions make her paranoid. There was no "him."

Zoe forced her attention back to the cooking class that was drawing to a close. There would be time enough to check out the others in the class during the tasting that was to follow.

But when the class began to sample the food, she saw no one she could assume might have been her watcher.

Maybe she was going round the bend.

Having lost her appetite, Zoe decided not to stay for the tasting. Outside the Cordon Bleu, she was getting her bearings as to which direction the nearest metro station lay when she felt someone tug her arm.

"Mademoiselle . . . mademoiselle." A small boy shoved a bouquet of fresh flowers and a white embossed box into her arms, then started to leave.

"Wait . . . I . . . who?"

The young boy turned and pointed to the flower stall. *"Ce monsieur."*

There was no one at the flower stall but the old woman who sold the flowers.

The boy looked surprised, then scurried off into the crowd.

The old woman at the flower stand continued to smile. Zoe waved and started toward her. *"Madame qui . . . le bouquet?"* she asked with her limited French.

The old woman shrugged to indicate she did not know.

"Merci." Zoe handed her a tip anyway.

As soon as she was out of sight of the woman, Zoe tossed the bouquet of flowers into a trash receptacle. Flowers held bad memories. Her husband had used them as hollow apologies whenever he'd worked too much. She was also tempted to do the same with the white box, but decided instead to save it for Lauren-Claire to open, knowing she would get a big kick out of this latest development.

As she rode the metro back to the apartment, she speculated as to who her secret admirer might be. With her luck, it was probably the little old man in the beret she'd sketched as a French king.

Or was it the man with the long dark hair and wide shoulders leaving the metro? She glanced around the crowded car, but no one fitted the description.

Having a secret admirer was flattering, even exciting. She shook off the little thrill that traveled up her spine at the thought that it was also a little dangerous.

"See, I knew I was right!" Lauren-Claire exclaimed with a smug nod, when Zoe told her about what had happened at the cooking class and showed her the square, flat, white-embossed package.

"What's in it?"

"I don't know. I saved it for you to investigate."

"What? How could you carry it all the way home and not look inside the box?"

Zoe shrugged.

"What if it were a bomb?"

Zoe let the package slip from her fingers and drop to the sofa. "Yeeck!"

"I was kidding. Can I open it?" Lauren-Claire asked, reaching for the package, her dark eyes shining with excitement.

"Sure."

Slipping off the lid carefully, she shoved the tissue wrapping aside and whistled. "Whoever he is, he's got yummy taste…Agnès B." She read the label as she lifted a pink mohair cardigan from the box.

"Glad you like it, it's yours."

"No way. This is a gift to you. You have to wear it *first*," she added with a grin.

"I'm not wearing it."

"I know, you can wear it tonight."

"Tonight?"

"Right. Remember the students I met on the metro the other day? Well, I sort of promised them we'd meet at the Bus Palladium tonight. You'll come with me, won't you? I'd hate to go there alone."

"What is the Bus Palladium?"

"It's the club where *everyone* goes."

"I don't know, Lauren-Claire. I'm a bit old for that crowd."

"Oh listen to you, *Grand-mère*," Lauren-Claire joked. "You aren't even thirty yet."

"I feel thirty when I'm around you."

"You'll feel twenty if you come watch the dancing. Say you will, please. It's my last night in Paris before I leave on holiday, you have to come."

"Oh, all right," Zoe agreed, knowing she'd regret it.

"Cool."

"But I'm not wearing the sweater."

The Bus Palladium was jammed, and after an hour or so Lauren-Claire gave up on finding her new friends. Instead she opted to go to another nearby dance club, which turned out to have enough room to mingle and see the dance floor.

"Aren't you glad I talked you into wearing the sweater? Pink looks so fine on you," Lauren-Claire said as they stood watching the crowd.

"It's shedding all over my black jeans and everyone I pass," Zoe grumbled. "I don't know why I let you talk me into these things. I feel like I'm asking for trouble by wearing it."

"Trouble? What are you talking about? It's only a sweater."

"So why do I feel like it has strings attached? Strings that are even now being pulled by the puppet master."

"Ah, but a *très* gorgeous one, no?"

"Hey, Lauren-Claire . . . why did you leave the Bus? We saw you leaving." The lanky Irish university student Zoe remembered from the metro was heading toward them with his two friends.

When the three young men reached them, the music blaring over the loudspeakers took on a decidedly Latin beat.

"Ah, the forbidden dance," the Irishman said, wiggling his eyebrows. "Come, you must dance with me, *chérie*." He took Lauren-Claire's hand and led her to the dance floor.

"Would you like—?" one of his friends asked, but Zoe cut off his request with a quick shake of her head, sure she would be arrested for corrupting the morals of a minor from the look of what was going on out there.

"I really don't know how," she said with a smile, not wanting to offend.

"I could teach you, *mademoiselle*," a low, sexy voice whispered from just behind her ear. "That is, if I were to forgive you for trashing my flowers."

She was certain when she turned the phantom wouldn't be there, but turned nonetheless—gasping when she saw dark hair skimming broad shoulders.

"You're the one who's been following me!"

He said nothing, just stood there in cowboy boots, jeans and Harley T-shirt.

"Why don't you leave me alone?"

"The sweater," he said, ignoring her demand, his eyes lingering on her curves. "You wore it."

"A mistake." She turned away, dismissing him.

"I don't think so. You look very beautiful in it," he whispered near her ear, his breath warm and sexy on her skin.

"Go back where you belong."

"Dance with me." It wasn't a request.

The two university students beside her were clearly oblivious to their exchange; their eyes were glued to the short skirts and sexy underwear that showed when the women moved in the risqué dance.

"I don't want to dance with you."

"Do you want me to make a scene?" he inquired, with quiet deliberation.

No, she didn't want that. It was Lauren-Claire's last evening before her holiday and Zoe didn't want to ruin it, so she allowed him to lead her onto the dance floor.

She nearly choked at his next demand as he caught her up in his arms. "Spread your legs . . . about two feet apart," he instructed, wrapping one hand around her waist and taking her hand in the other.

"You're kidding!"

"Do it." His intense look brooked no argument and she followed his instruction. Thank heavens, she was wearing her black denim jeans and not the short skirt that had practically become a uniform since her arrival in Paris.

Just when she thought things couldn't get any worse, they did.

"Now . . . straddle my thigh," he said, beginning the South American dance that was as hot as molten steel and as provocative as the glint in his blue eyes.

Zoe glanced around and saw what he was instructing her to do was really part of the dance. Too late, she realized she should never have worn the sweater, never have let Lauren-Claire talk her into coming here. Most of all, she should never have come near a dance floor with him.

The dance was at first embarrassing, then irresistible. She didn't want to think about what the sexy, sinuous moves were doing to her libido. She didn't have to imagine what they were doing to his. They were dancing extremely close—pelvises brushing.

The song seemed to go on forever, circuitous with no natural end. She felt as if they had been dancing far longer than she knew they had in fact. Oh, no! Now he was beginning to shimmy to the beat, coaxing her traitorous body that wanted even more. The sultry rhythm of the music matched the fire in her veins.

She was too old for this. She was going to have a heart attack and die. And then die again when they put the cause of her death in her obit.

Zoe gave up. She lost herself to the music and the man.

The puppet master pulling the strings. Her strings. All the right strings.

Embarrassment flew out the window along with her inhibitions as she gave herself over to the dance. Allowed herself to do what she'd come to Paris to do.

Live.

"Ahem . . ."

Zoe looked up into amused blue eyes. "The dance is over, *mademoiselle*."

"Oh." She felt her face grow scarlet.

"So, do you still want me to go away, *chérie?*" he asked, a knowing look in his eyes, a confident strut in his voice.

"Yes," she croaked, then turned and fled.

2

"SO YOU'RE FINALLY AWAKE," Lauren-Claire observed when she returned to the loft around noon after a morning shopping trip—a last-minute indulgence before she left on holiday.

"I thought I'd go with you to the airport to see you off," Zoe said with a yawn, looking up from the magazine she was thumbing through absently. It was a French *Vogue*, so all she could do was look at the pictures.

"Great. Hey, wait till I show you what I bought at G. Rodson for my trip."

"G. Rodson?"

"It's the name of a shop on rue de Chartres, specializing in *beaux vêtements* . . . stuff worn by Hollywood male stars in the forties, fifties and sixties." She held up a jacket. "Isn't it cool? It used to belong to Gary Cooper."

"I don't think it's going to do much for the cowboys back home," Zoe said, looking at it doubtfully.

"Well, what should I wear, then?"

"You got anything in gingham?"

Lauren-Claire looked aghast. "You're kidding, right?"

"I'm kidding. What you're wearing right now is fine." Lauren-Claire was wearing her short black skirt and ballet slippers. "Besides, with eyes like yours, you don't have to worry about a thing. Don't be surprised if they make you register them as lethal weapons when you go through customs."

"Zo-o-e."

Zoe continued to tease. "The cowboys back home don't have a fighting chance. With your eyes and French accent, they'll be lassoed, hog-tied and eating French toast before they know what hit them. Come on, let's get you on that plane."

"Let me get my bag. I've only got one, since everything I packed is black."

Not everything, Zoe thought, smiling to herself. While Lauren-Claire had been out on her last-minute shopping spree, Zoe had wrapped her pink angora sweater in tissue and slipped it into Lauren-Claire's bag.

"Oh, there is one more thing I need to know before we go."

"What's that?"

"Where to send bail money...."

"Zo-o-e." Lauren-Claire socked her in the arm as they left to hail a taxi for the airport.

It wasn't until they were waiting for Lauren-Claire's plane to be called that Lauren-Claire brought up the subject Zoe had been hoping to avoid.

"So you finally met your mystery man last night, no?" she said, taking a sip of the soda she was holding. "That was some dance the two of you were doing!"

"I don't want to talk about it," Zoe said, sulking.

"Okay, okay. But you do have to admit I was right. He is *très* gorgeous, isn't he?"

"Yeah, *très*," Zoe grumbled.

Lauren-Claire's flight was announced and the subject of Zoe's mystery man was dropped in favor of getting Lauren-Claire on the plane.

"Oh, I almost forgot." Lauren-Claire stopped and searched through her purse. "I bought something for you while I was shopping this morning, but you'll have to pick it up. Here's the address of the boutique and the receipt."

"Lauren-Claire... you shouldn't have," Zoe objected.

"Nonsense, I wanted to. Now give me a hug and wish me a good holiday. When I return we'll visit my family. They're all dying to meet you."

Zoe gave her a hug, wiping away a tear. She was going to miss her friend over the next two weeks. "Speaking of dying, that's just what your family is going to do when they meet Billy Joe-Bob, their future son-in-law, when you bring your cowboy home with you."

"Who said anything about marriage?" Lauren-Claire replied blithely, handing her boarding pass to the attendant and giving Zoe a quick wave and a wink before she disappeared.

ZOE LOOKED at the address on the bit of paper Lauren-Claire had given her, then up at the address on the bistro she was passing. According to the bistro's number, the boutique should be just ahead.

For an overcast afternoon there were a lot of people out on the streets: students with Walkman headsets, old men heading for a game of boule, and young mothers hurrying along with their small children.

Not a broad-shouldered man in a leather jacket among them.

Yet she kept looking. She'd been shocked last night, but if she were to be honest, she'd have to admit she'd secretly liked being pursued by him...had liked his sexy recklessness.

He was nothing like the husband she'd left at home.

Ah, here it was, number eight. Zoe stopped outside the small boutique. Pulling out her compact, she applied a shade of bright red Chanel lipstick she'd treated herself to at the Chanel boutique. One couldn't be in Paris without having something by Chanel. While the lipstick wasn't inexpensive, it was the only Chanel article she could afford.

Looking into the compact mirror, she smiled. The bright red color gave her a confidence she didn't feel. While she didn't know what to expect inside the boutique, she was working on not letting the French shopkeepers intimidate her.

Taking a deep breath, she pushed open the door. Inside the walls were painted a glossy deep pine green, an almost perfect match for her eyes, she thought. The long suede sofa and scattered plush ottomans were in a dark eggplant color. On one wall hung a large rug in a contemporary motif, while the pickled wooden floor beneath her feet was bare.

The whole look of the boutique was sleek high tech. And she didn't have a clue as to what they sold.

Zoe swallowed dryly. So much for not being intimidated.

"May I help, *madame?*" a chic older woman asked in a soft but assertive voice.

Why do I feel like she's inferring I'm in the wrong place? Zoe wondered.

"Yes, please." Zoe handed her the receipt Lauren-Claire had given her.

"*Oui*... I will check. Please wait one moment."

The woman returned a few moments later with a package.

"Follow me, *madame.*"

Zoe followed her into the hall to three adjoining dressing cubicles.

"Please try it on, *madame*," the saleswoman said, handing her the package and pointing to the spacious cubicle. "The garment has been selected especially for you and we will take care of any alterations, should you wish them."

"Thank you." Zoe took the package and entered the cubicle.

The cubicle was as sparsely furnished as the rest of the boutique. Evidently less was more when you had money. In one corner was a rattan and Rilsan chair painted a vivid purple. Beside it on the wall was a Lucite shelf holding one Japanese iris in a chrome vase.

Zoe moved to study her reflection in the mirror that took up an entire wall. Her image didn't fit the sleek surroundings, though she liked the way she looked.

She was wearing a rayon wrap dress in a tiny print pattern and over it a cotton jean jacket with the sleeves rolled to her elbows. The skirt of the dress hit her at midcalf. On her feet were white anklets and white baby-jane sandals.

There was that feeling again.

She spun to the doorway, startling the saleslady who had entered with a cup of coffee. "*Excusez, madame,* I thought you might like a *renversé.*" Setting the delicate cup and saucer upon the shelf, she explained. "It's a Swiss version of coffee with milk that our regular customers are fond of." Bowing out, the saleslady said, "I'll be back to check with you a little later, *madame.*"

The music piped into the dressing cubicles was smoky jazz and Zoe's body unconsciously responded to its lure. She began swaying to the rhythm as she opened the package containing Lauren-Claire's surprise.

Lifting it from the package until the tissue wrapping fell away, she smiled and shook her head. Lauren-Claire truly was incorrigible, she thought, studying the red leather bustier decorated with gold studs. It was the hot item of the new decade. Intended as outerwear, the elaborate and sumptuous bustiers had become all the rage. She'd seen several at the Bus Palladium and then later at the other dance club they'd gone to, where . . .

She couldn't possibly wear it.

Not in public.

Could she?

Glancing up, she caught her reflection in the mirror and saw herself swaying to the provocative music. She looked again at the daring bustier in her hands and decided she should at least try it on. Dropping it onto the rattan chair, she gave herself over to sweet fancies and began to flirt with her reflection in the mirror . . . began undressing to it, as if for a lover. Imagined *him* watching as she shrugged out of her cotton denim jacket.

Posing prettily, she let her hair swing forward, giving the mirror a peekaboo smile while she slowly began unbuttoning her soft, clingy dress. As the dress fell away, she plunged heedlessly into fantasy, imagining intense blue eyes flowing over her like slow, warm syrup. Her body began to heat, making her feel as if she were lying on a beach with the sun kissing her bare skin . . . the sand tickling in curious places. . . .

She placed her hands upon her body, slowly running them along her curves, arousing buried thoughts and secret yearnings.

Peeling down the top of the lacy bodysuit she wore beneath her dress, she reached for the red leather bustier. Lowering her eyelids sleepily, she walked to the mirrored wall as if in a trance. Listening to the hot jazz, letting it take control of her movements, she trailed her breasts over the mirror's cool surface, pebbling her nipples into a pale blush.

The pupils of her green eyes were soft and dilated as she stepped back from the mirror. She was breathing shallowly as she wrapped the bustier around her backward, catching the zipper and starting it up before tugging the garment around to shelter her breasts.

Reaching one arm over her shoulder to her back, she pulled at the zipper, edging it up until it stuck.

She tugged harder, but to no avail.

"Can I help you with that?"

Zoe jumped and whirled to the doorway—to see *him* lounging there.

"Are you crazy? How long have you been standing there?"

His eyes touched her body in a silent caress while he remained in the doorway as if he hadn't a care in the world.

"You . . . you . . . can't . . . you must leave," Zoe stammered nervously. "Quick, before someone discovers you. What were you thinking?"

His eyes glittered with desire. "You really don't want to know what I was thinking . . . or perhaps I should show you. . . ."

"No!" Zoe stepped back. "You must leave. Now."

He began walking toward her. "Don't worry, *chérie*. It's okay. I told the saleslady I was your husband." His cocky grin could have sold Yankee blue in Dixie.

"You didn't—"

"I surely did." He nodded, plainly unrepentant. "Any chance I could talk you into showing me some wifely affection . . . not that you look all that wifely in that . . . Well, whatever it is, it's hot," he said, his body tense. "How do you feel about temptation? Ever give in to it?"

She swallowed dryly, watching him warily.

His lips were a whisper away. "Come, *chérie*, wouldn't you like to press your sweet body as close to me as you just did to that cold mirror? I can assure you I'm much hotter."

She slowly shook her head, but knew she lied.

His hands went under her chin and he pulled her out to the middle of the room, turning her to face the mirror. "Let's see how we look together."

He stood behind her, slipping his fingertips just beneath the lace-trimmed edge of her bodysuit's high-cut legs, causing her to moan softly as desire began to burn inside her.

Her breath came in quick pants when he placed his warm hands flat against her hipbones and pulled her back against him. He was firm and hard as he moved her in slow, sensuous circles against him.

She had no will of her own as she waited in fascination for his next command.

"Turn around."

She faced him. He reached inside the gold-studded bustier and palmed her breast, his thumb teasing her nipple.

His lips lowered onto hers as he uttered a fierce growl and she allowed his tongue to bury itself in the damp cavern of her mouth.

His left hand tangled in her cascade of golden brown hair and anchored his ravenous kiss, while his right hand withdrew from her bustier to slide itself over her bottom.

Caressing the back of her thigh, he lifted her leg and brought it around to rest on his hip. Her head began to spin when he rubbed himself against her, fitting the proof of his need into the cleft between her thighs.

She felt him lift his head to look into the mirror at their reflection as she melted against him.

"How are we doing back here?" the saleslady called out cheerily.

Zoe sprang away from him.

"By the way, the lipstick was a perfect match...when you still had it on..." he said with a sexy wink as he turned and left the cubicle.

Seconds later she heard him say to the saleslady, "A perfect fit."

3

AS ZOE SAT WAITING to order her dinner at the new bistro Lauren-Claire had recommended, she glanced furtively around the tables. She was being stalked.

What she didn't know was how she felt about it.

Was she being lured into the dangerous liaison of her wildest fantasies? And if so, was she going to allow it to happen, or was she just playing with the idea and nothing more? Had her fantasies brought him to her? Perhaps it was he who had sensed her thoughts and sought to bring her fantasies to life.

Why was she thinking such reckless thoughts... thinking of taking such a risk? He was sexy, enticing...temptation itself. How could she not yield when it...*he* was what she wanted.

She'd barely slept at all last night.

And when she had, she'd thrashed about in the throes of dreams full of dark, erotic images. Unfulfilled longings she'd kept suppressed during her marriage.

The waiter interrupted her thoughts, setting her drink before her. "I will be back shortly to take your order for dinner," he promised, going off to deliver the rest of the orders on his tray.

Zoe took a sip, letting the soothing drink work its magic. Was it Paris that was freeing her inhibitions? she wondered. Or was it *him?* This man she didn't know at all—but in whom she recognized a matching wildness. A wildness she felt at his every touch . . . at his glance.

A matching desperation.

Looking down, she fiddled with the napkin. She was wearing Lauren-Claire's gift beneath her jean jacket. And the Chanel lipstick. He'd been right—it was a perfect match. Restlessly she crossed her legs, hearing the whisper of the essential black hose she wore with her short black skirt and flat black shoes.

She almost looked French—except for her hair. Unlike the short cuts on almost every woman in the bistro, her hair was a thick mane of soft, golden brown. Her manicured fingers twirled a luxuriant strand as she wondered where *he* was.

Maybe the flirtation was already over.

"*Mademoiselle*, this gentleman's name is Grey—"

"Don't bother with introductions, André, the lady knows I'm no gentleman." The words, uttered in a low, raspy drawl from an aggressively sensual mouth, resonated with confidence.

The waiter gave a Gallic shrug and moved off.

Zoe looked up at the man who'd arrogantly cut off the waiter's attempt at an introduction. It was *him* lean and lithe, his stance that of a street fighter with ballet training.

His clothes reflected the same dichotomy; the aviator jacket new, the jeans ancient and ripped in scandalous places.

"So you got up the nerve to wear it. But not without a jacket, eh?" he said, slouching into the seat opposite her, assessing her openly as he set his beer upon the small table between them.

She didn't flinch at his leisurely perusal. Instead she took a sip of her drink and glanced again around the trendy bistro, making a pretense of ignoring him.

She'd been expecting him, yet he'd surprised her by boldly joining her without invitation. She was feeling several emotions all at once, fear, anger, excitement and danger.

Lifting his beer to his lips, he continued to study her profile through half-shuttered eyes. His abrupt words cut into her pretense. "I thought we might eat to-gether...."

She studied him a moment, then turned her head to the entrance of the bistro, as if she expected someone to arrive.

"I know you aren't expecting anyone. Your friend is on holiday and . . . and there will be no other man."

The intensity of his burning blue gaze engulfed her. "What . . . what is it you want?" she challenged him.

"I want . . . what you want," he answered, his sexy voice crawling along her spine as he covered her slender hand with his sculptured, strong one.

The act was intimate . . . dominant.

"We're total strangers," she objected, pulling her hand away. "You don't have the slightest idea about what I want."

He didn't like the fact that she was going to be difficult, she knew as he tried to mask a scowl. He meant to
have her, it was there in his eyes. He might slow the pace
of intimacy by luring her throughout a leisurely meal.
But when the meal was finished, he meant her to leave
with him.

Willing or not.

"Roast chicken and steak *pommes frites* sound good,
don't you think?" he suggested, glancing at the menu
written on the mirrored wall.

She didn't answer.

The man called Grey signaled the waiter to return to
their table. Placing their order, he nodded to her anise-
and licorice-flavored drink. "Would you like another?"

She shook her head.

"Nothing for the lady, but I'll have another beer."

When the waiter nodded and moved off Grey turned
his attention back to Zoe. "Why Paris?" He lighted a
Gitane and the action drew her attention to his incred-
ibly sexy mouth; the hard line of his upper lip softened
by the plush sensuality of the lower one.

"I'd rather you didn't smoke."

"So would I," he agreed, taking the cigarette from his
lips and crushing it beneath his boot.

"You didn't answer my question," he said.

She shrugged.

His eyes lingered on her a moment. "Perhaps with
your artist's eye for color you wanted only to capture

the pale sunlight, the cool grays, the red-tiled roofs and the blue of Paris skies."

She didn't answer. She couldn't. She was lost in the blue of his eyes.

"No? Well then maybe you've come to Paris to see the Cadre noir horsemen in their black uniforms and tricorne hats appear in public for the first time in three centuries...."

She remained silent.

To hell with slowing the pace of intimacy, he seemed to decide as he leaned in to reclaim her hand. Lifting it to his lips, he raked his straight white teeth back and forth across her knuckles, the act deliberate... intimate and provocative.

"I have it.... You've come to Paris to experience its intoxicating sensuality." His voice threw down a velvety soft gauntlet.

Simmering animal magnetism flared between them with all its raw power; their bodies communicated on a primal level.

"I'm right, aren't I?" he said, compelling her to answer as he turned her hand in his, sliding the flat of his tongue across her palm.

Her breath caught.

"Tell me..." he coaxed, blowing the damp path his tongue had swept with his warm breath. "Tell me your...desires."

Swallowing with difficulty, she lowered her eyes to the table separating them, breaking the erotically charged moment.

When she looked back up, she'd regained her composure. "I desire you to leave me alone."

"You're lying. If not to me, then to yourself. Did you lie to your husband?" Awaiting her reply, he nibbled at the V between her thumb and forefinger.

"I . . . I don't have a husband. I left him."

"Why?"

She avoided his eyes. "Because he didn't love me enough."

He released her hand and tilted her chin with his forefinger so she would have to look at him. "Then he was a fool."

She looked away. "His career became his mistress."

"I wouldn't make that mistake," he assured her, his words a vow.

The hot look he gave her robbed her of the power of speech.

"Come on.... You can't tell me I haven't been in your thoughts. That you aren't wondering right now what I'd be like if I really wanted to stir you up . . . if I lost control...lost myself in you. Are you afraid that I might do everything right? With strangers there are no inhibitions...."

"You aren't serious," she said. "No one takes those kinds of chances."

"They do if they live for love. If they go with their sexual longings. You want to, I can see it in your eyes. You want to tremble with wanting. Don't you think I can bring you to such abandon . . . the freedom you felt when you were skating, the wind caressing your body?"

"You don't know...."

"I can match you...follow wherever impulse and desire might take you."

Zoe picked up her drink and put it back down. She didn't know what she wanted.

And then he began stroking the inside of her wrist...slowly, significantly, his eyes never leaving her.

She clenched her thighs, and her earlobes began to tingle with warmth. She could barely breathe.

"What are you thinking?" he asked.

"What are you thinking?" she countered.

He smiled, a completely wicked quirk of his lips. "Truth?" he asked.

"Of course."

"I was wondering what that sexy top of yours would feel like pressed up against my bare chest."

"Oh!"

"Don't you ever have such thoughts ... even fleeting ones?"

"I...I...*maybe*," she admitted.

"Tell me something wicked you've thought."

"I don't...I couldn't...."

"Close your eyes if you're embarrassed," he said. "Or would you rather I closed mine?"

"You," she said, glancing around the crowded bistro. No one was paying the least bit of attention to them.

"I'm listening."

"I can't think of anything right now," she told him at last.

His eyes blinked open and he laughed heartily. "I believe you are a tease."

"I'm not. I just can't think of anything at the moment."

"Perhaps I can help you. Hmm... What kind of naughty thoughts might cross your mind?" He fingered the cleft of his chin as his eyes danced.

"I know." He snapped his fingers. "Yesterday you were dancing in the dressing cubicle. I think you were removing your clothes to an unseen audience, weren't you?"

Zoe blushed. "An audience of one."

"Only one, really?"

She nodded. "I was imagining I was undressing for one man."

"Who?"

She took a deep breath with her admission. "You."

"Well, that makes your decision an easy one, doesn't it?"

"My decision?" Pushing her hair back, she played nervously with the sliver of gold hoop piercing her ear.

"About being my mistress."

Her mouth dropped open. "Your... *mistress*."

He nodded.

"You are kidding."

"No. I am not."

"But..."

"What is it you're so afraid of? The idea of being my mistress? Or the fact that you're considering the idea at all?"

Zoe couldn't believe what he was asking her. Or the fact that she was considering it. She ought to throw him as off balance as she was. "I haven't said I was considering it."

"But you are." His confidence was infuriating. He was infuriating. She felt her own confidence diminishing.

"Have you had ... lots of ... ah ... ?"

"No."

She said nothing, silence loud between them as they measured each other.

"You are the only woman I have ever desired to keep."

"And you are mad. How could you think I'd ever listen to your outrageous proposal, much less agree to it?"

"Because I can give you something no other man can. I can free you." His long fingers drummed on the paper tablecloth as he watched her trying to deal with the situation, watched her trying not to be fascinated with the very idea of it.

She closed her eyes, trying to calm her rapidly beating heart, thrilled with the very idea of his suggestion, her offense a pretense. Maybe she didn't want to know who she really was ... what she really wanted. Maybe she was toying with a puzzle that could never be put back together once taken apart and examined.

Or maybe she'd found the missing pieces.

The chemistry between them swirled with white-hot images and intimate longings. "Consider it," he coaxed. "Consider what it would be like to share our hidden selves, to explore our intimate boundaries...our darkest, most private secrets."

His whispered plea grew urgent with the force of his impatient desire. "I must have...I want you. *Desperately.*"

The waiter came with their order, set it before them, then moved off. The food issued a tantalizing invitation, though not half as tantalizing as the invitation he had extended to her.

He sat waiting, watching her. Hunger was etched on his face. Physical hunger that had nothing to do with food.

Zoe glanced across the room.

A woman dressed in a white cotton shirtdress and ivory linen jacket sat reading the latest bestseller about Coco Chanel while feeding tasty tidbits from her plate to the dog curled in her lap.

Then Zoe returned her attention to the provocative invitation awaiting her refusal.

Or acceptance.

She watched his sculptured hands lift a bite of the crunchy, browned roast chicken to his lips, left-handed in the Continental fashion. His eyes closed as his lips slid the bite from his fork. She watched him savor the unique flavor of the chicken served in its own pan gravy. His lips were hard, sensual.

She swallowed.

And so did he, his eyes drifting open.

Silence hovered between them like an uninvited guest at dinnertime.

He continued eating, pretending not to notice her covert study of him. She'd lined her eyes with a smoky kohl. The brassy light of the bistro glinted off her red, red lips like a danger signal.

Zoe finished as much of her meal as she could manage in the tensely erotic atmosphere. Finally laying aside her fork, she blotted her lips with a paper napkin and asked, "Isn't what you're suggesting highly irregular?"

Pushing his plate away, he leaned back in his chair and smiled. "In the States, maybe. But in France...no."

She nodded on a small laugh. "You're right. I'm such an American."

"So," he said, taking a long swallow of beer and looking at her intently, his eyes questioning. "You are considering it, then."

"No, I merely meant the whole idea of a man taking a mistress. I thought it was traditionally a much older man who took a younger woman as his mistress. You and I, we are, after all . . ."

"Yes?"

"Contemporaries. Equals."

He shrugged. "So?"

"The trade-off in such an arrangement is usually the man's money and power for the woman's youth."

"You're right, of course," he said, his finger playing at the cleft in his chin again. "Ours would be a somewhat different arrangement. Still, in one important way it would remain traditional."

"I don't understand," Zoe said, toying with the napkin in her hand.

"The fact that we are equals does not change the fact that you must be prepared to submit yourself to me—totally."

"Submit . . . ?"

He nodded.

"But how is that equal?"

"It is for your own pleasure as well as mine."

"You can't believe that."

"It is the truth."

Angry she began to shred the napkin she'd been toying with. "What if I don't wish to cater to a man? What if I found that role to be unfulfilling?"

He reached to still her hand. "You are confusing me with the man you left because he neglected you. I've told you I would not make the same mistake. As long as you are my mistress, your wishes will also be catered to—by me. I will make it my business to see that you find your role to be . . . fulfilling."

She pounced on his words. "As long as I'm your mistress. . . . And how long were you planning that to be?"

"I don't know. We'll have to see, won't we?" he said, his leg brushing hers as he stretched. His boot kicked something lying on the floor beside her handbag. Reaching down, he picked up her camera.

"Nice camera." Looking at her through the viewfinder, he played with the automatic zoom lens. "Nice view, too. Would you consider posing for me? We could start with you fully dressed as you are now," he offered, his tone hinting at an erotic progression.

"Will you put that down!" Zoe demanded, flushing with embarrassment. It annoyed her that she couldn't tell when he was playing with her and when he was serious. Good heavens, perhaps he was serious about everything! Or maybe everything was play.

She shook her head, confusion reigning.

He clicked off a shot of her before putting the camera down. "I think we're going to have to work on the submission part of our arrangement."

"We don't have an arrangement," she reminded him with a tight smile.

"Right," he tossed back with male arrogance and a touch of boyish charm.

"Why don't you slip off your jacket and let me take your picture?" he coaxed, leaning close and running his finger lightly over the crests of her breasts spilling from the rigid bustier. "Damn, this thing is hot looking. . . ."

"Why don't you slip off your jacket and let me take your picture?" she countered, slapping his playful hands away.

"Touché," Grey said, giving up with a great show of reluctance. "New camera, I see. Did you buy it to take souvenir pictures of your trip to Paris? Or are you toying with the idea of photography as another career?"

Zoe's smile was sheepish, a bit shy. "I don't know. I guess I am toying with the idea. I wish I had been in Paris several months ago. The Galerie Montaigne's first exhibition featured Man Ray and I would liked to have seen it."

The waiter returned to clear their plates and inquire about dessert.

"Why don't we linger over *tarte du jour?*"

"What time is it?" she asked, returning her camera to its original resting place beside her handbag on the floor.

"The bistro doesn't close until midnight. We have plenty of time."

"I . . ."

"Indulge me."

Taking her silence as acquiescence, he ordered the *tarte du jour* for two.

The waiter returned with the open-faced tarts a few moments later, set them down with a flourish and left.

Blue eyes surveyed her from across the table. "We share a weakness for sweets. It will be interesting to find what other . . . um . . . weaknesses we have in common, don't you agree?"

"I haven't agreed to be your mistress," Zoe reiterated, starting on her dessert.

Grey lifted his fork to his mouth. "Haven't you?"

"No. I can't believe I'm even talking to you about such a thing. It must be Paris or the strange mood I've been in lately."

"Coward."

"I'm not."

She noticed something then. She wasn't lonely. She was having fun. Even wondering whether he was all an act or really desperate for her was . . . exciting. He was pursuing her like a man possessed.

Stalking her.

Seducing her.

Sweet-talking her.

And he was succeeding. She might resist a while longer, but she knew what the final outcome would be. She would go with him, because she would never be able to forgive herself if she didn't.

She had to give him a chance.

She had to give herself a chance.

It was a risk . . . but so was living.

"Want to know what I think?" he asked, breaking into her thoughts.

She waited, watching as he leisurely licked an errant crumb from the back of his fork, his knowing eyes assessing her.

"I think . . ." he said, puncturing the air between them with his fork, "I think you want to."

There was a hint of wickedness in his voice.

"Oh, yes, I think you want to real bad. This mood you say you've been in. You feel restless, don't you? Edgy . . . hot, even."

"I beg your pardon."

"Baby, you can beg for anything but my pardon and get it. Come on, I dare you. Or are you too afraid? Too afraid to chance exploring your intimate boundaries? Is that it? Are you too afraid to *know?*"

"I . . ."

He wasn't going to give her a chance to retreat to safety. "Consent to be my mistress for one week. With no running out, no second thoughts. If you want to call it over at the end of the week, so be it. I'll grant you whatever you wish."

She stared at him over the chasm of temptation. The lyric of a song played in her head. "...the devil had blue eyes and blue jeans." Closing her eyes, she leaped. "Okay."

He tilted his head slightly in approval of her decision. "See? That didn't hurt a bit." Lifting her hand to his lips, he brushed kisses over her fingertips, then signaled the waiter for the check.

After paying it, he led her outside into the cool Paris night. He liked Paris best at night; liked the light and architecture . . . the mood.

Taking Zoe's hand possessively, he guided her down the sidewalk past the rose marble facade and tinted windows outlined in polished brass of the new Louis Vuitton megastore.

A bit farther along in their stroll, he turned down a cobblestoned side street, pausing beside a shiny black Porsche, sitting like a spider awaiting its prey.

As he inserted his key into the lock, a glint of something caught Zoe's eye. It was the moonlight glancing off a pair of silver handcuffs, dangling from the Porsche's rearview mirror.

4

ZOE FOUND the soft leather's caress against the back of her stockinged legs disturbingly sensual as she slid into the passenger seat of Grey's car.

Grey loped around to the driver's side as she glanced nervously around the basically black interior of the sports car. Instinctively running her hands along the edge of the seat, she failed to allay her anxiety or find a seat belt.

No one had to tell her Grey was a kamikaze driver. He looked far too comfortable sitting in the complicated-looking cockpit in his bomber jacket, his hands at home on the leather-wrapped steering wheel.

"What are you looking for?" he asked, as Zoe's hand continued searching.

"The seat belt. I'm sure this car is an open invitation to taking curves at breakneck speeds."

"Air bags," he explained, calmly putting the Porsche into gear. "One each."

"How comforting."

He glanced at her, his expression sardonic. "And here I thought you were throwing caution to the winds, coming with me."

"Maybe I'm having second thoughts," she said, glancing covertly at the rearview mirror.

"They aren't allowed," he replied, his words a warning as he turned his eyes back to the road.

The chestnut-tree-lined grand boulevards of Paris flew by; a blur of cafés, boutiques, museums and cinemas. As they left the city she caught sight of a gargoyle atop Notre Dame cathedral and wondered fancifully if the gargoyle were any relation to the man beside her. Well, at least in spirit—she had to admit the man sitting next to her had the patrician good looks of a wealthy vintner's spoiled heir—someone who raced cars to annoy his stuffy family.

As they left the brilliantly lit city behind them, the full import of what she had agreed to began to sink in. It occurred to her then that her recent mood of ennui had slipped over the borderline into insanity. "Where are we going?" she asked, a little late, to be sure, as they were already on the *autoroute;* glamorous, seductive Paris behind them, the French countryside ahead.

"The countryside where I've rented a château."

"Is it far?" She covered a yawn with her hand.

"Just go to sleep. I'll wake you when we arrive."

"I'm not sleepy," she lied. Zoe realized she was taking the biggest gamble of her life—and she didn't have the clothes for it. "We'll have to turn back. All I have is what I'm wearing. I don't have any of my things with me."

"Nice try, but no deal. I'll buy you anything you need. Now why don't you relax and try to get some sleep on the way?" he suggested.

Grey slipped a Michael Bolton cassette of romantic ballads into the car's sound system. The strains of the singer's heartrending, "How am I supposed to live without you?" flooded the car as she laid her head back against the seat.

She could tell they were going very fast, though she felt only a fraction of the car's power was being used. Like the man driving it, the car seemed to have a vital reserve.

Glancing back at him, she thought he seemed to be at one with the rhythm of the car. She admired the light touch of his fingertips on the wheel as he took the corners smoothly. Her eyes moved to the large speedometer gauge centered next to the tachometer in the cockpit—and just as quickly looked away. There were some things it was better not to know. They flew into another turn and she experienced a sense of exhilaration when they exited the tight corner—the car and the man's composure were phenomenal.

Grey opened the sunroof and the sweet wine scent of the countryside filtered into the car. Feeling oddly coddled, Zoe fell asleep, not waking until she felt herself being lifted by a pair of strong arms.

"What...where...what are you doing?" she asked, pushing against his hard chest and blinking her eyes groggily.

"You were sleeping," he explained. "I decided to carry you rather than wake you."

"We're there...already?" Squinting in the darkness, she could just make out the steeply pitched slate roof of the château and the dormer windows. As Grey carried her up the stone path toward the front door a heady scent assailed her nose, causing her to sneeze.

Grey's chuckle was low as he bent to unlock the oak front door. The ancient door's window was decorated with intricate iron grillwork. Shouldering his way inside, he carried her effortlessly.

Switching on a lamp, he headed for the stairs.

Zoe noted a French Renaissance-style table near the door and had a fleeting glimpse of vaulted ceilings and slate floors as they passed a couple of Louis XIV armchairs and several gilt-framed paintings.

"I can walk, you know," she said, when they reached the top of the stairs.

"Now you tell me, after I've carted you all the way up here." Making a mock pretense of being winded, he set her down in the upstairs gallery and opened the bedroom door. The light he switched on when they stepped inside shed a soft glow over the faded cotton print covering the bedroom wall.

"Make yourself at home." He handed her the camera and handbag he'd slung over his shoulder. "I've a few things to attend to downstairs."

Crossing the room, Zoe set her handbag and camera upon a painted satinwood writing desk inlaid with decoration. The fancy iron bed nearby, dressed in white lace-trimmed linens, looked as softly seductive as a new bride.

Her thoughts, however, were decidedly unbride-like. Steamy, sweat-slicked lovemaking; those were the

images her mind was painting when she thought about
the way Grey looked at her.

Decidedly unbridelike thoughts, yes. But perfect
thoughts for a mistress. Had she really agreed to such
a thing?

On her way to the alcove in the bedroom housing the
porcelain metal ball-footed tub, she stopped at a skirted
dressing table. She studied her reflection in the mirror,
thinking she should look different somehow. But no,
she didn't look particularly wicked. She looked like an
average American woman with clear blue eyes and long
tawny hair. She looked classic, confident even . . . not
at all wicked.

But she felt wicked.

Grey had been right about her feeling edgy and restless. Having slept on the drive out from Paris, she was
wide-awake now, though a little travel weary. What she
needed was a bath; a long, lazy, decadent soak.

A lavish assortment of scented oils, powders and
soaps filled a pretty basket set next to the tub. A heated
brass towel rack beckoned with its thick, warm towels.
Giving in to the idea, she turned on the tap.

When she walked back to the bedroom and began
undressing, she could hear Grey moving about downstairs. She wondered what he was doing as she laid her
sweater, T-shirt and short skirt upon an old wicker
chair, draping the black hose she peeled off over the
back of it, as well. Was he opening the curious assortment of packages she'd seen on the table on their way
up the stairs?

What could be in them? she wondered as she walked naked to the tub. Her hair swung forward as she added scented bubbles beneath the splashing faucet. Retrieving a plastic-coated rubber band from her handbag, she pulled her long tresses into a makeshift ponytail without the aid of a mirror. Wispy tendrils escaped and she blew them from her face as she stepped into the tub of warm, fragrant water.

Sliding down into the rounded tub, she felt the enveloping water's soothing caress and swished her legs back and forth to create undulating waves. Reaching for one of the scented soaps, she worked up a rich lather and used a natural sponge to slick it over her damp body, scrubbing busily until her skin glowed.

Then, scooping handfuls of water, she rinsed off the creamy suds. Cleansed and tranquil, she leaned back, letting relaxation seep over her while her mind drifted off—her eyes slowly closing as she thought about why she was there and what she wanted.

Why she was there was the easier question to answer.

She'd come because the person she'd been before she'd married would have come. Before she'd willingly assumed a subservient role in her marriage, she'd been an adventurous person, curious and unafraid to take risks. As a teenager she'd often had to pick the lock on the front door to let herself out—or in—after hours.

Her husband, being a cop, had been paranoid about her safety. While he hadn't exactly kept her under lock and key, he had expected her to remain at home, a traditional wife. It had been a role she'd gloried in at first, but it had come to chafe.

What she wanted was the harder question to answer.

While she hadn't been happy or fulfilled in her marriage, she had to admit the life she was leading in Paris was also lacking. What she needed was some sort of balance.

The balance of a relationship that allowed growth but provided nurturing. She had a lot to give and needed someone open to receiving and exchanging affection, emotionally as well as sexually.

By taking action, she'd come alive and in the process had perhaps allowed herself to be seduced by darker yearnings. She realized she was following a path paralleling her husband's.

He'd been seduced by his career, a job that allowed him to explore the darker side of his nature. If she were perfectly honest, she would have to admit part of her husband's appeal had been his profession.

Yet while he'd been growing and changing, he'd expected her to remain the same. They'd been almost children when they'd married, neither of them knowing a lot about each other or about life. Back then they hadn't known or begun to explore who they really were. Puzzling over the riddle of who she was, she drifted off to sleep.

THE FOLLOWING MORNING Zoe awoke in the fancy iron bed in the bedroom of the château. Rising on her elbows, she surveyed the room, ascertained she was alone and that it was morning. Peeking beneath the sheets, she saw she was naked. And her clothing was gone.

Where were her clothes? For that matter, how had she gotten into bed? The last she remembered was being in the bathtub.

Winding the smooth white sheet around her, Zoe went to the tall casement windows dressed in filmy lace panels and discovered the windows were bolted shut. Apprehension prickled her spine as she glanced down to see a courtyard below paved with cobblestones. Beyond the courtyard lay a garden with formal beds, gravel paths and a fountain. Moving to another window, she looked down past the gray slate shingles of the steep roof to discover beds of French lavender lining the stone path to the entrance to the château. The clean sharp scent of the lavender was no doubt the cause of her bout of sneezing upon arrival.

Her eyes narrowed at her next discovery. The black Porsche they'd arrived in still sat out front. The rearview mirror had lost its adornment, however.

Leaving the windows, she made a search of the room for her clothes, even going as far as to check the wicker laundry hamper in the alcove. She came up empty-handed. And the door was locked—from the outside.

Was she a mistress or a hostage? Tugging the trailing sheet around her, she plopped onto the bed in frustration. Her rash decision hadn't left her with many options, it seemed.

Even if the windows hadn't been bolted, the pitch of the roof was too steep to climb, not to mention that she was on an upper level of the château.

Besides, naked she wasn't going anywhere, passport or no.

Her passport . . . She looked around the room again. Sure enough, her handbag, containing her passport, was missing, as well.

Her eyes lingered on the armoire in the corner, admiring its rich veneer. Perhaps there were clothes inside she could borrow.

Tugging the sheet closer around her, she went to retrieve a hairpin she'd seen in the bath alcove. The armoire was locked, she knew, from her search for her clothes.

Working impatiently—patience never having been one of her virtues—she managed, with a few well-chosen adjectives, to pick the lock. Pulling open the large, intricately carved door, she found an array of delicate articles hanging inside.

She fingered the exquisitely detailed lingerie arranged on a row of padded pastel hangers. A pretty antique-white cotton Victorian gown with a lace-trimmed bodice, tiny buttons and a flounced hem caught her eye.

Dropping the sheet she was wrapped in, she removed the gossamer cotton gown from the hanger and slipped it over her head. Thus dressed, she continued looking through the treasure trove of femininity she'd uncovered. Every item was in her size.

The garments ran the gamut, all the way from a wicked pair of black satin tap pants with demi bra, decidedly kittenish pale pink hipster panties and matching cropped tank top to a frankly provocative flip of sheer white garter belt with matching bra and panties.

Stacked below in the bottom of the armoire were tissued boxes of stockings in all colors and styles, socks and an antique wooden box with a tiny lock.

For a moment she considered trying her luck at picking that lock, as well. In the end she decided against it—picking the armoire's lock had been justified by her need for something to wear—picking the lock on the wooden box would be nothing more than giving in to her nosy streak.

She'd just closed the door on the armoire when she heard movement outside the bedroom and Grey stepped inside. "Time to rise and shine, sleepyhead," he called out cheerfully, crossing to the tumbled bed.

"Where are my clothes?" Zoe demanded.

Turning to face her, his eyes roamed over the Victorian gown appreciatively. He grinned ruefully and shrugged his wide shoulders. "I see you're resourceful."

"Where are my clothes?" she repeated, standing her ground, straightening ever taller, her action thrusting her breasts against the filmy gown that fluttered around her with feminine enticement.

His gaze grew soft and seductive, the room airless.

"I asked you a question," she blurted, willing to try anything to destroy the encroaching mood of intimacy.

"So you did," he agreed, shaking his head. "Your clothes, wasn't it? Let me see.... Yes, I remember. I sent them to be cleaned."

"Oh." She stared at the floor, momentarily lost for words. Looking up finally, she asked, "Do you intend to keep me locked up?"

"That's up to you." He crossed to her, rubbing the back of his hand along her jaw, his eyes trying to penetrate her reserve.

"I hardly see how," she objected, pulling back from his touch. "After all, you're the one with the key."

"A mere physical device. You have a more mystical key that circumvents my physical one."

"I do?"

"Yes. Pick the right outfit from the armoire and we'll see."

Zoe's stomach picked that inopportune time to growl insistently.

"Good, you're hungry. Come, I've prepared breakfast for us."

"Like this?"

"Why not? You look lovely."

"But . . ."

"I'm afraid, I insist."

Taking her hand possessively, he led her downstairs. The slate floor was cool beneath the soles of her bare feet as he guided her past the living room, through the dining room and out the tall French doors to a small terrace.

She was charmed in spite of herself, her spirits lifted by a bird singing in the rose garden. It was impossible to remain angry in such beautiful settings with a man who'd gone to the trouble of laying out an exquisite repast for her pleasure.

After seating her in one of the antique, twisted blue metal garden chairs, which looked as if it had come from an old-fashioned ice-cream parlor, Grey took his seat opposite her. His eyes held a pleased-with-himself look.

Zoe surveyed the white-linen-covered round table between them laid out with vintage china. Warm croissants lay wrapped in an embroidered cloth in a small basket, fresh strawberries sparkled dewily in a glass dish alongside a pitcher of cream, a bowl of sugar and a silver pot of melted dark chocolate.

"I thought we'd talk," Grey said, pouring tea from a matching china teapot.

"Talk?"

He nodded, spooning sugar into his tea.

Zoe looked out over the garden filled with pastel roses, their fragrance carried on the occasionally stirring gentle breeze to where they sat on the terrace, warmed by the sun's morning rays. She was more aware than she wanted to be of how the sun kissed his bare torso. He too was barefoot and wore nothing more than the familiar ancient jeans.

Lifting her teacup, she took a sip, then looked at him over the rim. "Is that what you usually do with your mistresses—talk?"

"I've told you, I've never had a mistress before," he vowed, setting down his teacup with force enough to rattle the matching saucer.

She set down her teacup as well. Reaching for a plump strawberry, she dipped it into the warm, melted dark chocolate and popped it into her mouth. Her eyes closed in delight at the slick, rich taste. When she opened her eyes a few moments later, Zoe gazed searchingly at her companion.

"What did you want to talk about?" she asked, taking another sip of tea.

Grey broke apart the flaky croissant he'd taken from the basket, then looked directly into her eyes.

"I've been wondering...."

He hesitated, the apparently made the decision to continue. "Did you ... did you enjoy your husband's lovemaking?"

Zoe coughed, nearly choking on the tea. "What?" she asked, unable to believe what she'd heard.

"I was wondering.... Was that the reason you left— because you didn't feel fulfilled sexually?"

"I ... ah ... I told you I left because ..."

"He didn't love you enough."

"I don't want to talk about this."

Grey spooned chocolate from the silver pot and drizzled it in a lazy pattern over his warm croissant. "As you wish," he agreed with an amiable shrug. Lifting the croissant to his lips, he licked at the chocolate before taking a bite of the flaky pastry.

Zoe swallowed dryly.

"Why did you lock me in?" she asked, finding her voice.

"I wanted to be sure you would be here waiting when I returned from fetching breakfast. You see, I wanted to surprise you, not the other way around." His eyes studied her. "You do have a history of running."

"I agreed to be your mistress for a week, you can trust me."

"Can I? How long did you promise to be your husband's wife?"

"That's different."

"Is it?"

"Yes. He broke the vows."

"Which . . . love, honor or cherish?"

"Most especially cherish . . . he left me in spirit long before I left him physically. I loved . . . I told you I don't want to talk about this," she said, and after wiping her lips with her napkin, fled to the rose garden.

Grey swore and hurried after her.

The gravel path in the rose garden hurt her bare feet. When she stepped on a sharp bit of gravel, she dropped onto a carved wooden bench with a cry.

"Did you hurt yourself? Let me see," Grey said, reaching her side and kneeling before her. "Here, I'll make you feel better," he promised, taking her bare foot in his hands. He began rubbing his thumb gently over the angry pink spot the bit of sharp gravel had scratched. Lowering his head, he kissed the spot, then continued planting soft, sweet kisses upon the tender arch of her foot.

"Don't," she said, pulling her foot away.

Grey reached for something beneath a rose bush. He stood up, holding a garden hose and turned on the faucet to send the water through the hose. "Here, this will soothe the sting," he said, letting a trickle of water spill over her bare foot.

"That tickles," she said with a girlish giggle.

"Mmm..." Grey murmured, his eyes growing mischievous as if with a provocative idea.

Turning the nozzle at the end of the hose until he got the fine spray he wanted, he gave her no warning. Aiming the hose at her, he raked the spray of mist across her thin cotton gown, wetting it. Within moments it was as transparent as cellophane.

When she would have covered herself from him, he turned the spray toward her face. Shrieking, Zoe placed her hands over her eyes. His laugh was rich and deep.

He turned the spray once again onto her gown, sweeping it back and forth over the bodice until her nipples puckered into hard pebbles erotically outlined by the wet cloth.

"Don't," she said, knowing her cheeks were stained crimson.

"Don't?"

"I don't want..."

"Oh yes," he disagreed. "I think you really do."

"Please."

"I want you to do something for me," he said, turning the hose away from her and adjusting the nozzle once more, this time to a much harder mist. He lowered his head and took a drink.

"What?"

"I want you to raise the hem of your gown for me."

"You what?"

"Now," he said, his voice firm and unyielding. "I want you to raise the hem of your gown now."

"You're not serious."

"Do it."

."But . . ."

"Do it."

She followed his command, lifting the gown a tentative few inches to midcalf.

"Higher."

She inched the gown slowly to her knees.

"Higher."

"I . . ."

"Do it."

She followed his direction, lifting the hem of the gown to midthigh.

"Come on. . . . You know what I want you to do," he coaxed, his whispered urging hoarse and sexy.

"I don't want—"

"Yes," he interrupted. "Yes, you do. You know you do. Come on, show me how pretty you are. I want to see."

Taking a deep, tremulous breath, she shook her head, keeping her knees clamped tightly together.

He laughed then, a rich, wicked chuckle as he perversely rained a mildly stinging mist across her knees. "Come on, *chérie*...move them apart for me...pretty, please," he whispered as a cloud momentarily hid the sun, throwing them into shadow.

She continued to refuse and he shook his head in mock sorrow. "My, my—you're much too shy for a proper mistress. We're going to have to work on that." His voice was low and full of sensual promise as he added with a wink, "After all, I did promise to make you feel better, didn't I?"

5

HE'D GONE AND DONE IT again!

Zoe tugged impatiently at the locked bedroom door. It didn't budge, not a fraction. Kicking it, she let loose a very imaginative combination of Anglo-Saxon words about Grey's unmitigated, colossal, not to mention macho nerve.

This was too, too much.

No way was she about to let him get by with locking her in the bedroom of the château a second time. Where had he gotten the idea that she was malleable, wanting only to please? He certainly hadn't gotten it in the rose garden, though she'd been almost tempted.

He was charming, of that there was no question. But charm was one thing, arrogance quite another.

Frustrated, she sat down on the bed, glaring at the locked door that was her host's handiwork.

When her temper had cooled a bit, she noted the Victorian gown she'd peeled from her wet body and left lying on the floor was missing. He must have slipped upstairs when she'd been toweling off in the bath alcove, taken the gown and locked her in with the stealth of a cat burglar.

She didn't know what kind of game he was playing, but she didn't intend to follow his rules—or to spend her days dressed in a towel. Going to the window, she looked down to find the Porsche missing. He'd gone off and left her locked away until he returned. Well, the days when she waited for a man's return were over. Not that she'd ever waited all that patiently. But she had waited. One time too many.

First she'd see about something to wear. Then she'd set to picking the lock on the bedroom door. After all, she'd gotten into the locked armoire, hadn't she?

The armoire . . . She remembered suddenly about its contents. No wonder he'd gone off unconcerned about her freeing herself. The only things she had to wear were the things in the armoire, and while they were exquisite, one could hardly call them . . . Well, she couldn't wear them outside!

Moving to the armoire, she slid the padded hangers back and forth, looking at her choices.

She settled on the black satin tap pants with demi bra. Stepping into the tap pants, she found their tulip wrap sides hit her hips provocatively. The matching demicup bra lifted her breasts, but only partially covered them.

The shimmering black satin material came to just below her nipples, displaying their lush pink tips like some courtesan's court gown of long ago. It was impossible not to be intensely aware of her sexuality while wearing the black satin that flaunted her body's sensuous curves. She felt certain it was the very reason the frothy wisps of satin had been selected.

The contents of the armoire must have come from the pile of packages she'd noticed when they'd arrived at the château. After all, he did have the key to the bedroom, enabling him to come and go as he pleased.

Moving to the decorative dressing table, she studied her reflection in the mirror above it.

"Mirror, mirror on the wall, who's the barest one of all?" she asked whimsically, looking dreamy-eyed and indulging in the sensations she felt at seeing so much of her translucent skin on display and in contrast to the black satin. Zoe saw a flush creep over her skin, revealing her embarrassment at being turned on by the way she looked.

So much time was normally taken up with the daily routine of living that one's sexuality was mostly denied and relegated to a back burner, something to be enjoyed only at certain briefly scheduled times rather than being an integral part of living.

Sighing, she retrieved the same bent hairpin she'd used to pick the lock on the armoire. How much harder could one lock be than another to pick? she rationalized as she set about the task on the solid oak bedroom door.

This lock, however, was much sturdier and a lot more difficult to crack. Compared to the armoire, the bedroom door was Fort Knox. Picking it took a much greater amount of her determined persistence, the utilization of her most colorful verbal adroitness and the sacrifice of a manicured nail. But in the end her perseverance paid off and the bedroom door yielded to her campaign.

As she exited, she felt as if someone were watching her and then realized it was all the animal-head hunting trophies mounted on the wall. She continued to the top of the stairs then stopped, beginning to have second thoughts about exploring the château. What if someone were about? She looked down at her skimpy attire; she was hardly dressed to meet anyone. No, she decided, there wasn't any danger of that. After all, this wasn't a house party. This was something else entirely. Just what, she wasn't yet sure.

Descending the stairs, she peeked into the living room off the entry hall. The room was shadowy dark with small-paned windows and thick walls of stone. She could just make out exposed beams and a large fireplace holding court in the center of the room, surrounded by surfaces of chestnut and oak.

Moving a bit farther down the main hall, she took little note of the dining room, her curiosity having been appeased when she'd passed through it earlier on her way to the terrace for breakfast. Just ahead, off to one side, she could see a large open doorway to the spacious kitchen and its profusion of hanging greenery, an odd assortment of baskets and gleaming copper pots suspended from a rack over a huge scarred wooden table.

It was two tall carved double doors to her right however, that caught her attention. Going to them, she found the doors unlocked. She'd located the library, as was obvious from the row upon row of books inviting her in. Yes, she decided, a book would distract her until her host returned and they had the little talk she had planned for him.

Venturing inside, she began moving along the shelves of books in the dark-paneled room. The walls of built-in bookshelves housed an extensive and wide-ranging collection, and she browsed through them for quite some time. A small group of leather-bound diaries tucked away in a corner finally caught her eye. Selecting one, she carried it to the sofa with her.

Switching on a nearby lamp, Zoe curled up on the sofa among the plush brocade pillows. It was a very masculine room, with a globe as big as a beach ball mounted on a brass stand, and antique crystal liquor decanters locked in a glass cabinet behind the massive desk.

Stretching languidly, she reached to adjust a pillow behind her back. She knew and femininely enjoyed the fact that she looked racy, lying about in these refined surroundings in the midnight-black satin undies, her still-damp hair pulled up on her head in an old-fashioned topknot, drying tendrils fluffing about her face. The soft glow from the lamp lent a peachy fire to her skin. Lying there she looked petted and pampered . . . she looked a mistress.

Was it her imagination, Zoe wondered, or were all the characters in the books on the library shelves gossiping about her in hushed whispers?

GREY STOOD in the library doorway. A small, leather-bound book lay open beside the sofa; it had clearly slipped from Zoe's hand when she'd drifted off. She looked alluring, elegant and soft to the touch. Her gentle curves burned a permanent picture upon his mind as he watched her sleep. He had an overwhelming temptation to give in to tactile pleasures, but fought it; he had yet to complete Zoe's surprise.

Some time later, he showered and changed, then returned to the library and the still-dozing Zoe. He crossed the room to kneel beside her, brushing a whisper-light kiss upon her lips. Indulging himself further, he blew soft gusts of air across the full tips of her blush-pink nipples until they hardened. There was a rustle of satin as she shifted in her sleep, smiling at some private delight. He wondered what she was dreaming of.

Picking up the book that had fallen from her hand, he moved to sit across from her in the leather wing chair. Absently opening the diary he began reading the feminine hand that had put some very naughty Victorian fantasies to paper.

Some minutes later he felt someone watching him and looked over to see that Zoe was awake.

"That book . . . that's where you got the idea for all this, isn't it?" she whispered.

"Perhaps," he answered noncommittally, closing the book and smiling at her without repentance.

"I hope you don't think—"

"No, I don't think—I know."

"I'm not . . ." she objected further.

"Yes . . . you are."

"But . . ."

His look silenced her.

"Why are you dressed like that?" she asked, eyeing him suspiciously. He was dressed rather formally. His shirt and pants, even his shoes were white. The sea of white flannel set off his tan and made him look nineteenth-centuryish; poetic, even.

"I'd like some tea," he said, his imperious manner indicating he not only wished to be served, but fully expected it.

"I'd like some clothes," Zoe countered, sliding into a sitting position on the sofa, adjusting the pillows about her in a bid at concealment. The brocade pillows and the brevity of her dress made her feel like a pasha's concubine—captive and cosseted. The effect excited her, but she had come to Paris to become a modern woman, not an old-fashioned one. How had everything gotten so out of control?

"You'll find the silver tea service and china cups and saucers in the dining room. I set them out on the oak sideboard. Tea and biscuits should be in the glass kitchen cupboards," he informed her, ignoring her request.

He smiled at her childlike pout, but his eyes widened at the adult malice in her eyes as she glared at him.

"Run along now and be a good little mistress. When we're through with tea, you can go up and dress in the new clothes I bought you."

"You're enjoying seeing me squirm, aren't you?"

He shrugged. "That is the general idea of having a mistress, isn't it?" he answered, purposely playing the double entendre she hadn't intended.

"I'm going up *now* and dressing."

"Zoe . . ." he called after her softly, stopping her in midstride. Turning, she saw he still retained control; in the palm of his hand lay a key.

"You'll only find your bedroom locked," he explained. "You may as well abide by my wishes."

She stood hesitating and looked at the key.

"The tea," Grey insisted, pocketing the key.

"But I'll look pretty silly, serving you a formal tea, barely dressed."

Rising, he strolled toward her, then walked around her, pursuing his prurient study. He took his time viewing the charms so enticingly displayed in the skimpy black satin. Finally, when she thought she might scream, he faced her once again. Lifting her stubborn chin with his long forefinger, he smiled wickedly. "Not to me," he answered.

She swatted his finger away. "Of course not to you, you're perverted."

"Really . . . ?" he asked, clearly amused.

"Quite."

He nodded as if considering her assessment of his character, then returned to the wing chair. "I'll have the tea anyway," he insisted.

Any way, was it? In that case, his lap was taking shape as a good place to serve it, as soon as she got the tea to the same boiling point she'd already reached.

"And if I refuse?"

"I suggest you don't," he answered. Picking up the journal from the table, he began reading, effectively dismissing her.

She wasn't to be dismissed so easily.

"Really? What is that, some sort of threat you're making? What? Will you send me to my room without dinner—no, wait, without my clothes, perhaps? Are you going to spank me . . . or maybe take away my nonexistent privileges?" she demanded, all sass and fire. Indignantly raising her hands to her hips, she nearly upset the applecart that was her skimpy French bra and spilled her apple-firm breasts. She quickly lowered her hands before her breasts tumbled at his interested gaze.

"You choose," Grey said seductively, appearing to be completely unaffected by her tirade.

"Oh! Never mind, I'll get your tea and crumpets, master," she said with all the sarcasm she could muster, turning away from his continued amusement.

"Now you've got the hang of it," he said, chuckling when she slammed the door on his chauvinist remark.

In the dining room she found a glistening Sheffield silver service and a set of matching teacups and saucers, china, hand painted with pastel nosegays. Setting everything upon a silver tray, she carried it off to the kitchen, where she found a well-stocked pantry. "Everything I need but the rat poison," Zoe muttered.

As the water heated, she thought about the situation she'd found herself in; it mirrored her marriage. Once again she was being domesticated, waiting on a man . . . seeing to his comfort. Once again the man was in control.

It had been thus all her life. She'd been raised by her aunt in a male-dominated, ethnic family. Her cousins had all been boys. The experience had had its plus and minus side. On the minus side was the catering to male needs and ego, on the plus side benign neglect. Since she was a woman and her aunt was older and tired, no one had bothered to indoctrinate her with beliefs.

Other than the day-to-day upkeep of the males in the household, she'd been pretty much left to fend for herself and to develop her own ideas about things. Before her marriage she'd been a pretty independent young woman. Alas, she'd traded that independence for affection. She hadn't realized it at the time, but her husband had expected her to behave in a certain way or he'd withhold his affection.

And since she'd so desperately craved being held—loved—she'd sacrificed her freedom. She'd thought there might be freedom in total submission to this dark stranger, but now she wasn't so sure.

The aroma of spicy tea wafted through the kitchen as she filled the teapot, then placed the tea biscuits on an Edwardian cake stand. Adding a pot of honey and white linen napkins to the tray, she carried it back to the library where the large rat waited.

"See, you can be quite domestic when you put your mind to it," he said, putting the diary aside.

Feeling like a Playboy bunny, she held her tongue, dipped her knees and rested the heavy tea tray on the coffee table between the sofa and the wing chair where Grey continued to sit.

"I'll pour," he offered to her surprise.

"You're sure it wouldn't be too much of a bother?" she asked ungraciously.

"I think next we need to work on your manners."

"There's nothing wrong with my manners—besides, I don't imagine there's anything in Emily Post on how to behave while having tea in one's underwear," she said, taking the cup of tea he offered her.

"Nonetheless, a real lady should be able to balance her teacup and saucer on her knee with or without clothes," he countered.

Rising to the bait, she tried, unsuccessfully, then set her cup of tea upon the coffee table after taking a sip.

Glaring at him, she said, "I guess I'm not a real lady."

"I'm glad to hear it," he observed, stirring a spoon of honey into his tea; infuriatingly, he managed to balance his cup on his knee. "Now, about my plans for this afternoon."

6

ZOE DESCENDED the stairs with trepidation. She was dressed all in white, as Grey had been earlier. The clothes he'd bought and laid out for her were decidedly old-fashioned: a flowing silk blouse whose buttons matched the strand of pearls at her slender neck, a long chiffon skirt that swirled at her pale-stockinged ankles, flats with grosgrain bows slippered her feet. She looked as innocent as the young girl in the gilt-framed painting in the hall, she thought upon passing it.

Standing just outside the library, she fidgeted nervously with a straw boater, then placed it atop her head, tucking a few fluttering tendrils of long curls behind her ears as she resettled the hat. Taking a deep breath, she entered the library where Grey waited.

She was making a conscious choice to continue playing out the game she'd willingly entered into with him.

Where would it end?

"Grey?" She didn't see him at first.

"So you're ready, then," he said, looking over his shoulder from where he was replacing the diary among the books on the shelf.

Ready? She didn't know about that. If someone had told her six months ago that she would enter into this bizarre liaison, she would have told them they were crazy. But then she wasn't the same person who had left her husband.

In fact she wasn't quite sure who she was. Or even why she was doing what she was doing.

When her unwed mother had died in childbirth, her course in life had been set. She'd grown up no one's child. When she'd met her husband, she'd reacted to his affection like a wilting flower to water. Living alone for the past six months had been lonely, so perhaps that was why she enjoyed Grey's obsession with her.

Whoever she was, she was allowing him to dominate her in the process of exploring her intimate boundaries as a woman. Boundaries she had repressed during her marriage.

"You haven't said where we're going," she said as he thumbed the spines of the matching diaries on the shelf before him.

"Going? We aren't going anywhere," he said, pulling another journal from the shelf and turning to face her.

"Then why am I dressed like . . . why are *we* dressed like this?"

He shrugged casually. "I thought you'd like it, that it would lend a certain atmosphere to our afternoon. . . ."

"You mean *you* like it—the playacting, the costumes, all of it. Don't you?"

"Don't you?"

She looked down at her attire. "Well, yes, it's very pretty, but—"

He stopped her, placing his forefinger to her lips. "Hush, you think too much. Just this once, don't think, okay? Just allow yourself anything. Grant yourself permission to yield to temptation."

His eyes—how would she ever be able to deny them anything?

Anything at all.

She nodded her acquiescence.

"Good. Come along then."

"Why are you bringing that journal along?" she asked.

"I thought we could read aloud to each other."

"From that!" Zoe exclaimed, her voice cracking.

"Don't be such a goose," he said, tweaking her nose. Taking her hand, he swept her along beside him through the hall and on outside. "I've got a surprise to show you," he promised, leading her down the path beyond the château.

She averted her eyes from the carved wooden bench and the garden hose still lying beside it like a sly serpent. She could feel color stain her cheeks as the scene replayed in her mind and was relieved Grey didn't appear to notice as she trailed along beside him.

"Have you no curiosity at all?" he asked.

"Curiosity?"

"About my surprise...."

"I'm not sure I even like surprises," she objected.

"Well then, humor me and try to pretend you like mine," he suggested when they came upon a hedge of tall cedars.

"Close your eyes."

"Why? What's this?"

"Just close your eyes and trust me."

Reluctantly she did as he wished and allowed him to lead her through the cedars.

"Okay, you can open your eyes now."

Zoe blinked, adjusting her eyes to the bright sunlight and saw a long rectangular grass court. The reason for the tall cedar hedge was explained: the cedars stood sentry, keeping wayward croquet balls from sailing into the nearby woods.

"It's lovely."

"Isn't it?" Grey agreed, as he set about putting up the game. "Imagine having a private croquet court tucked away like this." In short order he had the wickets all set up for a game.

"I bet they held family tournaments here with grand lawn parties," Zoe said, taking a practice swing with a wooden mallet.

"Do you know how to play?" Grey asked, striding over to select a red ball and its matching mallet with a red stripe near its base.

"Do you?" Zoe asked in return. A warm, gentle breeze swayed the tall cedars, bringing their scent to her as she selected the blue ball to match her mallet.

"Piece of cake," he bragged with a broad wink. "I've been reading up on it. You don't stand a chance, *chérie*. I'm going to wipe you all over the court."

"I wouldn't be so sure about that. I might be pretty good. I grew up with boy cousins."

"Yeah, but you're still a woman."

"What?"

"You're a woman," Grey repeated with a careless shrug. "That's why I'm being a gentleman and letting you go first," he said, stepping back and motioning her toward the double iron wicket one had to hit the ball through to start the croquet match.

She shot him a look of supreme annoyance, then gritted her teeth. Lining up her mallet, she hit the ball true.

"Well, I'll be damned, you are good."

"I told you," she said, missing her second shot.

"But not that good." He laughed at her miss.

"Want to bet?" she countered, wanting to take her impulsive words back the minute she'd said them.

"Do I get a handicap?" he asked, missing his shots.

"Only if you beat me," she muttered, smiling with sweet malice as she swung her mallet wickedly.

"But you're so much more advanced than me, you said so yourself."

"I am, aren't I?" she said, pleased as she passed her ball through the next wicket, only to set up an impossible position for the next shot, which she missed.

Upending her mallet, she leaned at an angle to the grass, using it as a makeshift chair.

Concentrating, Grey made his shot. "Okay, I'll take the bet without a handicap."

"Done," Zoe agreed when his next shot went wide of the wicket.

Leaning against his mallet, watching Zoe as she set up her next shot, Grey said, "Loser of the match grants the winner one wish."

"I'll be thinking on what my wish will be," Zoe said, not putting enough English on her swing, so that her ball rolled short of the wicket.

"I won't," Grey said to himself, pleased the afternoon was going to go as planned. It was time to resort to unscrupulous trickery. Dispensing with the chess aspect of the game, he stepped up to his ball and swung, sending Zoe's ball rocketing.

"You can't do that!"

"Oh, but I can. Care to have a look at the rule book?"

"But that's crooked."

"And where do you think the name croquet comes from, *chérie?* It means little crook . . . You know, as in by hook or by crook. The original mallet was a shepherd's crook and there has always been a crooked element to the game...it's part of its appeal. You can play the game and get someone's goat . . . so to speak."

"All this was in that book of instructions you read?"

He nodded smugly. "Want to know more about the history of the game?"

No, she didn't. What she wanted . . . what she really wanted was to take off her straw boater and sail it through the air at his head, like she'd seen one of the villains do with his steel-rimmed top hat in a James

Bond movie—but it would be such a shame to lop off such a lovely head.

In short, she wanted to beat him at his own game. She wanted to win so she could gloat—childish though that might seem.

She didn't win.

Even though she mounted a diabolical chase, she was outmalleted by Grey.

She wasn't a good loser, stalking off the croquet field to where he stood at the edge, holding his mallet over his head in victory.

He looked down at her sardonically. "Did you ever think your husband might have had some reasons for what he did?" Grey asked. "Or are you the sort of woman who insists on having things go her way?"

She took the thermos of lemonade he offered. "I wouldn't know what my husband's reasons were…he didn't talk to me."

"Perhaps he wasn't any good at talking. Most men aren't," Grey said, watching her sip from the thermos.

"This is good." She licked the corner of her lips with the tip of her tongue. "Where did it come from?" She handed the flask back to him, wiping her brow with the back of her wrist. "It's gotten warm, hasn't it?" A healthy color bloomed on her cheeks from the competition of the match.

"I brought it over with the croquet set earlier," he explained. "I didn't want to put you out after you'd gone through the ordeal of making me tea already to-day. Anyway, you're changing the subject," he observed, chugging down gulps of lemonade.

Zoe saw his throat working as a trickle of the tart drink slid down his jaw and dripped to mingle with a slight sheen of sweat on his tanned neck. She found herself wanting to lick off the trickling juice. "Stop it!"

"Okay, okay, if you don't want to talk about your marriage . . ."

"It's not that. . . ." She couldn't believe she'd voiced her thoughts. "Oh, never mind," she said, forcing her eyes away from his lips, which were still damp from traces of the citrus drink. "I'm going back. These clothes are hot."

He caught her wrist. "Not just yet."

"What?" she demanded, pulling her wrist free of his grasp.

He folded his arms in front of his wide chest and studied her. "There's the matter of the little debt you owe me."

"Debt?"

"Our bet. You lost, remember?"

"Oh that . . . yes, well, what is it you want? No, let me guess," she said, holding up her hand. "You want me to cook you a seven-course meal and serve it to you while wearing the black satin ensemble," she said smartly, making every effort to look bored.

His low, sexy words cut through the feigned boredom. "What are you wearing beneath these rather stifling old-fashioned clothes you're so anxious to get out of? What did you choose from the armoire this time?"

he asked, trailing his forefinger down the vee of her blouse until it rested on the first pearl button.

"I . . . ah . . ."

"Tell you what, why don't I show you the surprise I have for you and we'll talk about how you're going to pay your debt to me, eh, chérie?"

"But I thought the croquet court was the surprise. . . . It's so lovely and . . ."

"It's not the surprise." Taking her mallet from her, he placed it in a custom-made wooden chest. Closing it, he retrieved the small leather-bound journal from the ground, tucked it inside his shirt and scooped Zoe up into his arms.

"Gr-rey . . . ! What . . . ?" She clasped his neck and clamped her other hand on her straw boater to keep it from falling.

"I'm making up your mind for you," he explained, striding through the cedar hedge.

"Oh, just like being married," she muttered.

"Not quite, I don't think . . . you're my mistress, remember."

"Where are you taking me? Am I allowed to ask that, master?"

"Sure you can ask."

"But you're not going to answer me. As I said, just like being married."

"I'm taking you to the barn, all right?"

"The barn?" she repeated, seeing it in the clearing just beyond.

"Your surprise, remember?"

"Aren't you going to give me any hints?"

He appeared to consider the idea a moment, then said, "Okay, it's something I saw you admire while I was following you in Paris."

"Why did you follow me, anyway?"

"Perhaps I need a wife. Did you ever think of that?"

"Right, and perhaps I'm Sleeping Beauty."

"I'm counting on it."

"Oh, and I suppose one magic kiss from you and I'll awaken."

"Something like that."

She looked at him doubtfully. "About my surprise . . ."

"Well, it's something I saw you admiring when you were out with your friend before I approached you," he said, putting her down when they reached the barn. "Now, once again I'm going to ask you to . . ."

"I know, close my eyes and trust you."

"My, aren't we becoming a good little mistress!"

"I think that's an oxymoron," she said dryly.

"Watch it, I may decide to keep your surprise."

"And I may decide to let you, especially if it moos."

"Okay, you can open your eyes now," he said after leading her inside. It took a few minutes for her eyes to adjust to the dimmer light coming in through the windows, but when she did, she let out a cry of delight.

"It's beautiful! How did you know I've always wanted one?"

Grey laughed. "Because you were paying more attention to it than you were to me when Lauren-Claire was trying to point me out to you."

Zoe didn't pay any attention to him, she was tracing her hands over the exotic carousel horse. Dust motes danced in the sunlight filtering in the window, through which she could just make out the spring-fed pond beyond the low stone wall.

While the air was musty with the scent of hay stored in loose stacks in the rear of the barn, the area where they stood was empty except for the carousel horse.

"You like it, then?" Grey asked, coming up behind her, resting his hands upon her shoulders. It was a familiar, possessive touch.

She nodded her head, continuing to admire the exquisite creation. The white-and-gray horse looked rather like a knight's steed, festooned in pastel livery fit for a festival in times past. A time of chivalry.

The swirled-brass pole stand it was mounted on twinkled in the sunlight. The wooden horse was carved as if caught midstride, hooves up and flying.

"Is it really for me?"

"Yes, it's really yours," Grey said, chuckling softly at her excitement. Taking her hands into his, he rained gentle kisses upon the insides of her wrists to shivering, sensuous effect. His satisfied smile was bone melting as he looked at her indulgently.

"About our little wager..." he began, his thumbs rubbing lightly at her wrists.

Zoe returned his smile, anticipating that he would cancel her debt to him in the romantic moment.

"Yes?" She smiled up at him.

"Time to pay up," Grey said, reaching for the camera he'd placed on the floor by the window.

Her mouth fell open. "That's my camera. How did it get here? I don't understand...."

"I think you do."

"You set this all up, didn't you...?"

"That's right. I want to take a few pictures of you posing with your present. You don't mind posing for me, do you?"

It would be rude to refuse him when he'd gone to such lengths to please her. And truth be told, she was flattered that he wanted to take her picture. Flattered by the attention and companionship that had been sadly lacking in marriage.

"All right," she agreed, though a bit apprehensively as he activated the battery for the camera's flash.

"Come on, smile, *chérie*. At least pretend you're having fun."

"How many pictures are you planning on taking?"

"I only want to take a couple of you in that old-fashioned outfit. Consider it your present to me."

"Be sure and get a good shot of the carousel horse," she said, standing to one side of it.

"That's good, stay right where you are. Now lift your hand and rest it on the saddle...like that." He snapped the picture of her standing beside the horse, looking Sunday School innocent in her white finery.

"How about one of you up on the horse? Sitting sidesaddle," he said, when she looked down at her long chiffon skirt.

"I'll need a hand."

"Sure." Setting the camera aside, he came over to give her an assist onto the horse.

"How should we do this?" she asked, looking somewhat embarrassed and uncertain.

"Here . . . put your foot on my thigh," he said, bending his leg to give her a stepping place.

"I can't do that—your white pants."

"Don't be a silly goose. They already have grass stains on them from the croquet court. Besides, the cleaner's very good."

"Get a lot of grass stains on your pants, do you?"

"Nope. I usually wear jeans with the knee out, remember?"

She wondered what that told her about him.

"Okay—" she placed her foot on his thigh "—now grab hold of the brass pole."

She did as he said, grabbing the pole that ran through the carousel horse just in front of the saddle. He boosted her up.

Moving back, he picked up the camera once again and looked through the lens as she settled herself. The flash as he clicked off another picture caught her by surprise. Moving around her, he clicked off several more.

"I thought you were only going to take a couple of pictures of me in this outfit."

"Exactly," he said, going down onto one knee and clicking off another. "Let's try something else," he suggested, joining her at the horse. He ran his finger beneath the strand of pearls at her neck, toying with them . . . toying with her, she realized.

"Maybe you could take off your . . ."

"Oh. Yes," she said agreeably, eager to dissolve the suddenly torrid atmosphere. Purposely misunderstanding, she moved to take off the straw boater.

"No," he said, shaking his head. "I like the hat. Leave it on." His fingers moved then . . . down the front of her blouse, working slowly to undo the pearl buttons as he held her captive with his gaze.

Moving back, he picked up the camera once again, looking at her through the lens. "I'm waiting."

She took a deep breath, but did nothing further—made no move to follow his suggestion.

"The blouse, Zoe. I want you to take it off."

"I don't . . ."

He lowered the camera. "And your skirt."

"Grey, I don't think this is . . ."

"Zoe, look at the carousel horse. It's a bit of whimsy. How can you love it so and not want to be fanciful? To set the whimsy inside you free? Do it, Zoe. Do it for me."

She swallowed. "Turn around, then. Don't watch me, okay?"

"You're not serious?"

She sat waiting.

"Okay, okay," he agreed, throwing up his hands and turning so his back was to her.

Her clothing made a rustling sound as she maneuvered her way out of the skirt and blouse, dropping them onto the floor, where they made the scene look like a lovers' assignation, she thought.

"You can turn around now."

Turning, he saw her sitting primly on the carousel horse, her hands nervously clasped in her lap, the look on her face shy, yet some how wanton.

Grinning sexily, he snapped her picture. "I like what you decided on from the armoire," he said, his eyes appreciating the demicup sheer white bra, matching flirty garter belt and bikini panties set off by the straw boater, white stockings and bowed flat shoes.

"You know what I'd really like . . ." he said, winking at her.

"What?"

"I want you to pose for me . . . something provocative."

"Grey!"

"Come on . . . you know you want to. I saw you in front of the mirror at Madame Blanche's boutique, remember."

"That was . . ."

"Wanton, naughty."

"What do you want me to do . . . ?" she asked, hesitant.

"I want you to straddle the horse, for starters," he suggested with another wink.

"Turn around while I do it?"

"I'm getting dizzy with all this turning..." Grey muttered comically.

"Do it."

He laughed at her turning of the tables and did as she instructed. But he waited impatiently, tapping his foot to let her know it.

"Okay," she whispered a few minutes later.

He turned to the provocative vision. "Yes. Oh ye-eah..." he said, coming in with the camera for a close-up shot.

"Now take off your hat," he instructed. "I want you to look mussed—like you've just been riding."

Zoe did as he asked, setting the straw boater upon the carousel horse's head.

"Good. Now shake your head. Run your fingers through your hair. Mess it up. Yeah, like that. Make it look sexy. You've got the greatest long hair, you know. Don't ever get it cut. Never," he demanded, snapping a picture.

Then another.

And another.

"Grey, I think you've taken enough pictures."

"Just a few more...."

She didn't answer.

"One more, okay?"

"Just one," she agreed.

Setting the camera aside, he came over to her. "Here, let's undo your stocking." He eased his fingertip inside the top band of the sheer white nylon, where it was held by the frilly garter belt. With a flick of his fingers, he unsnapped it.

Warmth trailed down her leg as he eased the pale stocking down her thigh and calf to bunch it in a sheer cloud at her ankle in sexy dishabille.

Zoe ran her tongue over her dry lips.

"Yes . . ." he said, backing away and picking up the camera. "You look very naughty, *chérie*."

Grey's eyes were bright with desire as he instructed, "Now look at the camera, Zoe. Ahh. . . If you could see how the light looks on your skin. . . . Now, do one more thing for me. No, I'll do it," he said, coming to her. "Here, lean forward toward me and dip your shoulder just a little. Yeah, like that. Now, let me ease your breast out of one filmy cup here . . . a little farther. . . ."

He backed away, lifting the camera and once again looked through the lens. "Oh, yes . . . yes . . . you're beautiful, chérie. Okay. . . now I want you to place both your hands on the brass pole. That's right . . . now slide your hands up. Higher, reach up as far as you can," he instructed, watching through the lens as her free breast stretched into a taut peak. "That's good. Now I want you to roll your hips forward and dip your back. Oh, my. . . now look at me. . . look at me and say please. . ." he coaxed, his voice husky.

Zoe turned her head to the camera, trying to ignore the sensations the pose was creating, but the teeth biting into her bottom lip and the sultry look in her eyes gave her away to Grey.

The camera flashed.

"You must be out of film by now," Zoe said, her voice cracking. He'd carried her along in his excitement until she was drenched in the scent of what they were doing.

"Film . . . ? There's no film," Grey said.

"You're rotten . . . you know that."

His laugh was rich and lusty. Setting the filmless camera aside, he came toward her. "I think you deserve a dunking for that remark." Plucking her from the carousel horse and laying her across his wide shoulder, he carried her from the barn as if she were the spoils of victory.

"Put me down!" she cried, flailing her feet wildly.

"Cut that out," he ordered, giving her a swat on her soft bottom.

"Then put me down."

"I fully intend to," he said, laughing and stumbling as he carried her down the sloping path. When they reached the pond a rabbit scurried into a clump of nearby wildflowers and a flock of fantail doves fluffed their feathers at the disturbance the two humans were making.

"Grey, don't you dare," Zoe warned, when he rounded the low stone wall at one side of the pond and went to the edge of the water.

Ignoring her pleas, he began swinging her gently back and forth over the water.

"Don't worry, *chérie*. I'm going to join you in just a minute." With a final swing, he tossed her into the cool water with a splash.

Sputtering, she surfaced and began treading water, her hair streaming down in wet ringlets as she called out, "You really are rotten!"

"You said that already," he replied, shrugging out of his clothes until he stood on the bank naked, his body honed to the perfection of a marble statue. Taking a running jump, he leaped into the water, his golden body arcing in a clean, splashless dive.

He disappeared beneath the surface and Zoe didn't see him for a minute.

"Grey...?" she called, turning in the water.

A moment later she felt his hand jerk her ankle and yelped as he pulled her under the water, undressing her.

When they surfaced moments later, she'd gotten free and they were both beneath the low diving board that was mounted on the three-foot-high stone wall at the end of the pond.

"I've got an idea," Grey said, grinning wickedly.

"You stay away from me," she said, hitting the surface of the water with the edge of her hand, sending a splash of water into his face.

Grey slicked his hands back over his face and hair to get rid of the water, then began advancing upon her. The doves looked at him strangely as he began to cluck like a chicken to antagonize her.

"Cut it out.... Okay, what's your idea?" she asked, giving in.

"Can you manage to pull yourself up on the diving board?"

"What for? I can't dive."

"It doesn't matter."

She was still reluctant to leave the cover of the water. "I don't know...."

"Do it."

"But..."

"*Do it.*"

Looking around and seeing nothing but a few birds, she did as he requested.

"Okay," he said when she'd pulled herself up and onto the low diving board. "Now sit down and scoot out to the very edge of the board. That's right. A little farther."

"I'm going to fall in," she said, steadying herself as the board bounced slightly when he pulled himself up and knelt behind her.

"No, you're not," he said, steadying her and kissing the curve of her neck, water dripping from his hair to sluice down her front. "Look at our reflection in the water. It's like looking through a glass block."

"Mmm..." she said distractedly, studying the erotic picture they made.

"Stay where you are." He slipped off the diving board back into the water. His grin was wicked as he tread water just in front of the board.

"Lean back and brace yourself on your hands," he instructed.

"More mind pictures?" she asked, doing as he requested.

"Not exactly. Moving pictures are more like it."

"I don't understand."

"You will in a minute. Point your toes and stiffen your legs. Like that. Now open your legs and lower them until your feet dangle in the water."

Zoe gave in to the wanton sensation of cool water washing over her feet while the warm sun kissed her naked body.

Ducking his head, Grey dived beneath the water and came up at the very tip of the diving board, grabbing hold of it, his hands just behind where her buttocks rested on the very edge of the board.

"I'm slipping, Grey."

"That's okay, slip right here," he said, pulling himself up and placing his head between her thighs, his tongue laving her.

She took a quick breath and closed her eyes on a sigh, letting her head fall back. A moan escaped her lips as her neck arched and she gave herself over to the building heat his warm, damp tongue fueled.

Unconsciously, she lifted one leg and bent it, allowing him freer access. As she did so, his tongue slid inside her, bringing forth the sensation she was aching for.

AN HOUR LATER found them ensconced in the château's cozy library, polishing off a bottle of wine. Grey sat sprawled in the leather wing chair, wearing nothing more than his white grass-stained slacks. His bare toes played in the carpet as he drained his wineglass. Zoe wore only his abandoned white shirt. The shirttail skimmed her tanned thighs where she rested her empty wineglass as she lay stretched languidly on the sofa. Her head was cushioned by a nest of pillows.

Making a supreme effort, Grey leaned forward long enough to refill their glasses. "What?" he asked, seeing the considering look she gave him.

Zoe took a sip of her wine and studied him over the rim of her glass. "I was wondering . . ."

"About what?" he asked, settling back.

"Men," she said with a shrug.

He shook his finger at her. "Oh, no, you're not allowed to wonder about other men while you're my mistress."

"Who says?" she said on a warm, giggly laugh.

He glanced at the library shelves. "I read it somewhere. I think it was in a very thick book of rules for female behavior," he said, squinting as if trying to pick out the very book.

"Probably written by a man," she grumbled.

"Probably."

"Okay, since I can't talk about men in general, let's talk about you."

"Let's not."

She laughed. There was nothing more absurd than the joke nature had played on the sexes—making women verbal and men not. "Okay, then let's talk about men in general."

"What about men?"

"Well, for instance . . . do men have preconceived ideas about women and marriage?"

"Sure. Women want marriage."

"And men don't?"

"Yeah, after a fashion. But men don't think of marriage the way women do."

"So tell me, what do men think marriage will be like?"

Grey twirled the stem of his wineglass in his hand as he considered her question. Finally he said, "Most men probably want the tradition."

She glanced at him. "Tradition?"

"You know, fresh clothes, hot meals . . ." he grinned lasciviously ". . . great sex."

"All of this available on demand, right?"

"Of course."

She turned away from him. "There's just one thing wrong with that."

"What?"

"Everything."

"Okay, so what do women want?"

"Most women would like some control over their lives. You know, like a hot meal waiting for *them* . . . or great sex . . . the way they want it . . . a little romance. Why couldn't men sometimes put a woman's needs over their own, instead of taking them for granted? Why couldn't men sometimes be the care givers?"

"Is that what it would take for you to give marriage another try?"

"Is it too much to ask? Is it so hard for a man to allow a woman to be all she can be? What are men so damn afraid of, anyway?"

"Their feelings," he said quietly.

"Women have feelings too . . ."

The silence stretched out between them. Grey picked up the journal by his side. "We forgot to read to each other." He began paging through the journal.

"What are you looking for?"

"The good parts," he answered. He paused then. "Ah, here's one . . ." He pretended to read from the page. "She would make a perfect wife. He could tell by the way she kept her eyes downcast in his presence and never spoke unless spoken to . . ."

"That's not funny." Zoe threw a brocade pillow at him.

He dodged the pillow and continued reading out loud. "She was properly veiled and knew how to anoint his feet with oils."

"In your dreams." Zoe aimed another pillow that scored a direct hit.

Grey set down the journal and picked up the pillows, retaliating.

Within moments they were turning the library topsy-turvy in a raging pillow fight that dissolved into shrieks and rich, wicked laughter.

7

ZOE AWOKE the next morning naked once again. She had the feeling she was in a recurring dream. A very pretty one, though it seemed to be shot through gauze, as it was fuzzy around the edges. Then she remembered the bottle of wine. And Grey.

Who was he, anyway? Was he the cool, aloof charmer who had seduced her into agreeing to be his mistress for a week? Or was he the sweet, caring man who'd listened to her last night. A man who'd shown a sensitivity her husband hadn't. What did Grey want? What did she want?

She knew only what she didn't want. She didn't want a marriage like the one she'd had. Her husband had been a good man, but he'd neglected her. Love wasn't enough; it had to be tempered with a willingness to share and grow.

Rubbing her eyes, the room came into focus. Sunlight streamed in through the tall casement windows.

Looking over to the bedroom door she saw that it was closed, locked once again, no doubt. She was beginning to feel as though she was in a Gothic novel.

What was this thing he had about locking her in?

Surely he must realize he couldn't keep her, if she didn't want to stay?

Yawning widely, she stretched, the action causing the comforter to fall away. Shivering at the chill she resigned herself to the fact that the clothing she'd worn the day before wouldn't be in the room. She got out of bed to see what the armoire could provide in the way of warmth.

The best she could come up with was the kittenish, pale pink soft cotton hipster panties and matching cropped top.

After pulling them on, she rummaged around in the bottom of the armoire, eyeing the lock on the oblong wooden box. Holding out against curiosity, she picked a pair of matching slouchy pink socks instead of the lock. She felt only marginally warmer, as the thrust of her nipples against the soft cropped top showed.

Going to the dressing table, she studied her reflection in the mirror above it. She looked all of seventeen. As if determined to be perverse, she pulled her hair up into a ponytail.

A knock at the door surprised her.

"Come in," she called, going to sit down cross-legged on the bed.

The door opened. It hadn't been locked, after all.

Grey entered, carrying a white wicker bed tray. A mouth-watering aroma wafted from beneath the linen-covered tray.

Now this is my idea of room service, Zoe thought, noting he'd reverted to wearing washed-out jeans and not much else. And wearing them *very* well.

"You're up already. I had planned to wake you and surprise you with breakfast in bed." He raised his eyebrows. "I guess I've blown the surprise, huh?"

"No," she said, shaking her head. "I'm surprised. Where did an American like you discover the joys of breakfast in bed? Isn't it against the work ethic, or something?" Picking up the pale pink rose atop the linen covering her breakfast, she wondered if he'd known she would be wearing the pink undies she had on, or if the matching color was coincidental.

He laughed, his voice low and sexy. "I guess I must have a decadent streak in me that you bring out."

"Speaking of which, you didn't lock the door. . . ."

"I wasn't going anywhere." He knelt on the bed to set the wicker bed tray before her. "Besides, you'd just pick the lock again and get out."

"Aren't you cold?" she asked, trailing the pink rose across his bare chest.

"Not hardly. While you've been a layabed sleepyhead, some of us have been slaving over a hot stove."

She threw the rose at him and he caught it one-handed, showing very quick reflexes. "Now, now. Play nice, or I'll have to make you go back to bed without your breakfast," he admonished, stretching out beside her, propping his head upon his bent wrist.

"Let me see what's under here first," she hedged, lifting the linen cover on the tray.

"I could make the same request," he said, running his fingertip beneath the edge of her crop top that ended inches above her narrow waist, then seductively palming her breast through the soft material.

She slapped his marauding hand away. "I think you surpassed your weekly allowance for decadence yesterday. What's this?" she asked, uncovering a pile of colored ribbons along with a plate of cookies and a pot of tea.

"Sugar and spice and everything nice."

"My, what a lot of ribbons you have," she said, picking up the pile of colorful streamers and sifting them through her fingers.

"I bought some in every color. I wasn't sure what your favorite color was."

"How long have you had this ribbon fetish?" she asked on a laugh, picking up a jelly-centered cookie dusted with powdered sugar and taking a bite. Bits of powdered sugar touched her nose and sprinkled onto her crop top.

"Mmm . . . you look good enough to eat," Grey said, dusting the powdered sugar from her nose with the delicate petals of the rose, its sweet scent teasing her nostrils.

"About your ribbon fetish . . ." she reminded him, pouring a cup of the steaming orange spice tea into a flowered teacup.

"Oh, that. If you must know, there was this girl in fourth grade named Jennifer something or other who sat in front of me in English class. She had long hair that she wore in braids with ribbons on the ends. I used to tease her by stealing her ribbons. One day she cornered me on the school grounds and sort of beat me up."

"A girl beat you up?"

"I kind of let her. I mean, she couldn't really hurt me and I did have it coming. Besides, she was having such a good time of it, I didn't have the heart to try to stop her." He said it with such disarming charm that Zoe didn't know if it was a true story or an invention.

She took a sip of tea and considered him. "And ever since you've had a penchant for long hair, ribbons and—"

"A woman who gets out of control on occasion...."

"You know what I think?" she asked, polishing off the rest of the sugary cookie and picking another.

"What...?"

"I think you're full of it, that's what I think," she answered, licking at the jelly center, knowing what a provocative picture she made in her pink underwear, framed in the ruffled white bed.

"Do you, now?" He was silent for a moment, watching her. Pushing himself into a sitting position, he took away the cookie she was toying with. "You won't mind if I brush your hair out and braid it then, will you?" Having issued the challenge, he popped the cookie into his mouth, devouring it like Little Red Riding Hood's big, bad wolf.

She laughed. "Yeah, right." Did he really think she was buying his outrageous story?

"I'm not kidding," he insisted. "Come sit here," he coaxed, taking her wrist and leading her to the skirted dressing table.

"I'm *not* wearing my hair in little-girl braids," she objected.

"No problem. I graduated to French braids my sophomore year in high school."

"Still Jennifer?" Zoe asked, sitting down in front of the dressing table, not believing a word of it as she looked at his reflection in the mirror.

He grinned and winked. "No, Kirsten and Jill."

"You lie."

"Do I? Hand me the hairbrush."

Still not believing a word of it, she handed him the brush.

Releasing her hair from the ponytail, he began brushing it out until it settled in a soft cloud about her shoulders.

She watched him in the dressing-table mirror, giving herself up to the sensual stroking of his hands. Strong hands that could be gentle and caressing.

After a while he set aside the hairbrush and motioned to her to hand him the comb. Starting at the crown, he sectioned her hair into three even parts and began attempting to French-braid it.

His early efforts met with some success, but when he'd added several strands pulled from either side, he ran into trouble.

He started again with determination.

When it happened again on the second try, Zoe smiled openly.

By the third try, he was swearing beneath his breath and she was laughing out loud, having trouble sitting still enough for him to work as he began yet again.

"It's not funny."

"I think it is."

"Well, I don't. I'm telling you, I used to know how to do this. I *can* do this."

"Yeah, but in this lifetime?"

He shot her a pained look. "Wait, I know what's wrong."

"So do I—you can't braid hair."

"No . . . I can't braid dry hair. Let's go to the bathroom sink and wet your hair. I just remembered when I learned how to braid—it was on wet hair. I spent a lot of lazy summer afternoons swimming in the community swimming pool."

"With Kirsten and Jill."

"Right. The two of them were best friends and inseparable. They did absolutely everything together. Both of them were seniors...older women...and they sort of adopted me that summer. They thought I was cute."

"That made three of you," Zoe muttered, bending her head beneath the faucet so he could wet her hair.

He turned the water on full force, drenching her for her smart remark.

"Grey! Now look what you've gone and done!" The skimpy crop top was soaked, clinging to her provocatively.

"I'm looking, I'm looking," he said with a lascivious grin, holding the towel she wanted just out of her reach.

"If you don't give me that towel right now, I'm not going to let you braid my hair."

"Deal."

"Grey, give me the towel," she said, advancing on him. "Quit playing games."

He backed into the bedroom, holding the towel behind him.

She picked up the brush from the dressing table and threw it at him.

He ducked, avoiding it easily.

"Grey, give me the towel," she demanded again, enunciating each word slowly, her hands on her hips. "My hair is dripping all over me."

"I know." His eyes darkened and danced over her appreciatively.

"I mean it, Grey. Give me the towel."

He shook his head.

"Okay," she said, pretending to give in. Feigning a step to her left, she moved with deceptive speed and lunged for the towel.

She was fast, but his reflexes were faster. He dropped the towel and grabbed her, lifting her easily and tossing her onto the bed, rattling the contents of the breakfast tray.

"No!" she cried, trying to scramble away as he advanced upon her.

He was too quick, covering her and pinning her wrists above her head.

She squirmed beneath him, the action only serving to raise her skimpy crop top to expose the lower curve of her breasts.

"Get off me, you beast! You're going to upset the teapot!"

"Oh, you're not really concerned about the teapot being upset, now are you, chérie? Come on, admit it! What you're really concerned about is the sexpot being upset," he said, smiling down at her with a devilish glint in his eyes.

"I am not a . . . a . . . sexpot."

"Really?" He levered his long body for a quick, sweeping look down her disheveled one, warm and flushed from her struggles to free herself from him. "Couldn't prove it by me."

"Let me go," she insisted, trying to throw him off balance.

"Uh-uh. You wanted to play games . . . so we'll play games," he said, releasing her only long enough to reach for the pile of ribbons on the tray.

She immediately scooted up to the top of the bed and braced her back against the mound of pillows at the iron headboard.

"Wait, what do you think you're doing?" she demanded, trying unsuccessfully to twist her wrist free of his grasp as he knelt over her and placed it against the headboard, proceeding to loop one of the ribbons around both her wrist and the ironwork, effectively fastening her there with a pretty bow.

"You call this a game?" she asked, as he fastened her other wrist with a matching bow, despite her squirming efforts.

"I'm sure you've heard of it. It's called playing doctor," he said, playfully snapping the elastic of her pink panties as he got up from the bed and walked over to the satinwood writing desk.

"I don't remember playing doctor going like this..." she said, watching him pull up the chair from the desk and sit down beside the bed. "And now I suppose you're going to treat me to a sample of your warm bedside manner."

"Couchside manner would be more apt. I'm going to ask questions...very personal questions...and you're going to answer them. Just think of me as Dr. Sigmund," he said, leaning back in the chair and propping his bare feet upon the bed.

"Ah, *that* kind of doctor." She tugged at the ribbons tying her wrists, wishing her hands were free, so she could smack him. He was looking way too smug and pleased with himself as he sat there, drumming his fingers on his taut, flat belly.

"I guess I should consider myself lucky you haven't tied my feet," she said, looking at the soft pink cotton socks slouched at her ankles.

"I only do that if I have to resort to tickling to get the answers I want."

"You wouldn't." She looked at the ribbon ties again. She could probably reach them with her mouth, using her teeth to untie the bows and free herself—if she wanted.

She wasn't completely surprised to find she didn't want to. There was something nonthreatening and exciting going on between them. Despite the playacting, choice was involved. The pretty pastel ribbons he'd used to secure her wrists were satiny slick and would work loose with any effort at all on her part.

She knew it and so did he.

The pretense that they didn't was the sensual kick.

This then played to the dangerous limits of her wildest fantasies. It allowed her to surrender without responsibility to the lure of breaking through the bonds of convention to explore her intimate boundaries.

"What are you thinking about?" Grey asked.

"My husband."

"Your husband? Do you think that's proper protocol when you're with your lover? Should I be insulted? What were you thinking about him?"

"That he was a gentle, considerate lover. That he loved me...."

"And yet you left him...."

She nodded. "I left him."

"Did he ever do anything like this with you?"

She shook her head. "No."

"Did you wish that he would have?"

Zoe didn't answer.

"You secretly wanted him to, didn't you?"

She still didn't answer him.

"You should have told him."

She looked away.

"Look at me," he demanded.

"I can't look at you and talk about things like . . . like this."

"But you'd . . . look at me if I were to—" he leaned forward and trailed his finger down the inside of her calf and on inside her thick sock to stroke the arch of her foot. "—make love to you. . . ."

"Yes."

"I'm not going to, you know," he said, withdrawing his hand and leaning back in his chair.

"Why? Are you impotent?" she asked, turning back to face him.

His laugh was rich and lusty as he rose from the chair and stretched, revealing the power of his body. Walking to the window, he pushed aside the lace panel and looked down over the garden. Finally he glanced back at her.

"No. I'm not impotent."

"Then . . ."

"I wanted you to be my mistress for a week because I wanted to pleasure you, not me. I wanted to talk to you . . . find out what you want and need."

"Did Kirsten and Jill talk to you, those long, lazy summer afternoons?"

He nodded. "Yeah. I'd forgotten how it was, talking with a woman."

"Suppose I don't want to talk. Suppose what I want—what I really want is for you to make fevered, urgent, demanding love to me."

"It's not going to happen," he said, returning to slouch in the chair.

She turned away from him.

"Don't misunderstand me. It isn't that I don't want to, ah, ravish you. It's just that I'm not sure you know what you want. Maybe you're having second thoughts about going back to—"

"No. I know—" She bit her lower lip nervously. "I know what I don't want. I don't want to go back to a man making my decisions for me. I don't want a one-sided, traditional relationship, like the kind my marriage was. I was so young, maybe too young, when I got married. I didn't know any better, so I allowed it. I won't again."

"So you're saying your husband was too dominant."

"Everywhere but in the bedroom."

"So he wasn't any good in bed . . . that's why you left him."

"No. His lovemaking was tender and sweet. Wonderful, actually. . . but it's just that . . ."

"What?"

"Well, I always felt that he was following my lead. He never did anything. . . I don't know. . . he never seemed to get swept away by passion. He treated me like I might break."

"Maybe he was afraid. Did you ever consider that?"

"A cop . . . afraid?"

"Yeah, of hurting you, offending you, maybe . . . looking silly in front of you, even, by getting carried away," he suggested, moving from the chair to sit on the bed beside her. Reaching out, he began tracing a pattern on her bare abdomen with lazy indolence.

"A man would be afraid of those things?"

"Sure. What if he took the lid off Pandora's box, releasing his repressed longing and desires, and you were unable to fulfill them?"

"Have you ever thought there was a part of you that wasn't being fulfilled?" she asked, squirming as his hand wandered.

"I ask the questions, remember?"

"But that's not fair."

"Fair?" He lifted her foot and began tugging off her slouchy sock with his teeth. "It's my game," he said, beginning to kiss her instep when he had removed the sock. "If you don't like it, I'll take my ribbons and go home. Is that what you want?" He was nibbling at her soft rounded heel as his hand slid down her smooth calf to her inner thigh, where his fingers began toying with the edge of her high-cut panties.

Her "No," escaped on a strangled note when his long fingers inched farther. With her wrists still secured by ribbons, she was forced to accept the pleasure he insisted on giving her again . . . and again.

Who was he really? she wondered.

She did know one thing.

He was good with his hands.

8

ZOE CLOSED THE BOOK she'd chosen from the selection
Grey had brought up for her from the library before
locking her in the bedroom and leaving the château
once again. She'd had no intention of staying put, but
she wasn't in a rush to leave him soon, either. After he'd
left, she'd filled the old-fashioned tub with warm,
scented bubbly water and settled in for a long, decadent soak.

Once she'd picked up the thriller to read, she'd become engrossed, not even noticing at first when the
water grew cold. Feeling the chill, she'd toweled off and
lain across the bed to continue reading. The vampire
in the book was an enigma, not unlike Grey.

Now the sound of the car signaled Grey's return.
Setting the book aside, she got up from the bed and
went to the tall casement window. It was dark outside,
but she could still make out Grey's tall, shadowy figure in the moonlight as he walked up the lavender-lined
path in his bomber jacket and jeans, his arms full of
packages.

When he reached the front door, she turned away
from the window and went to the armoire to look for
something to wear. She was faced with only one op-
tion: a sheer white, all-lace camisole and matching

thong bikini. While the garments were exquisite, putting them on was only marginally better than wearing nothing.

She slipped them off the padded hanger.

Where did Grey go when he left her?

Kneeling before the armoire to rummage through the tissue-wrapped packages stacked in the bottom, she came up with a pair of white lace-topped thigh-high stockings to match the camisole and bikini.

While removing them from their tissue wrapping, she caught sight of the small, locked oblong box still in the bottom of the armoire. She'd meant to open it while Grey was out. Zoe promised herself she would find out what was inside the locked box at the next opportunity.

Who was Grey really? she wondered, slipping the camisole over her head, letting it glide down over her smooth shoulders to snag on her upturned breasts, then settle provocatively.

What did he really want with her? Was it only a week of uninhibited lovemaking? She pulled on the teeny thong bikini. He'd said he wanted her to be his mistress for a week—to submit to him totally.

What would happen when their week was up? Would he stay at the château...go back to Paris...travel around Europe...or would he return to the States?

And what did she feel for him?

Grey was dominant, yet understanding. He was sensitive to her feelings. But he also seemed unsure, as if he, too, were exploring what he really wanted,

needed. Perhaps he wasn't offering her security...
only adventure.

Paradoxically, she wanted both.

In the six months she'd been in Paris, she had enjoyed the adventure, but missed the security of her old
life.

In the days she'd spent with Grey she'd thrilled to his
exciting sexual games, but missed the unshakable faith
in her husband's love. While her husband had neglected her, he had loved her. In her heart she knew
that. Could a man who was willing to test limits... sexual boundaries, make the same promise of
faithfulness that was necessary to her?

Did Grey want marriage?

Did she want him without it?

Or did she only want a man who was somewhere
between the traditional husband she'd married and the
untraditional lover who was awakening her?

Did she want it all?

One thing she was sure of—she'd changed. She was
being herself, thinking and feeling all the things she'd
forced herself to repress in the past.

Now she knew for certain that no matter what she
decided, she would never go back to living a lie. The
man she chose would have to love her for who she really was.

Carefully scrunching the sheer white stocking between her fingertips, she slipped it over her toes and
smoothed it up her leg. After tugging the second one

firmly into place, she pirouetted in front of the mirror over the dressing table.

Her reflection was risqué; her hair had dried earlier in a tangle of wild abandon, and the brief, sexy lingerie made her look like the fantasy bride on top of a bachelor party cake.

Studying her reflection, she continued to muse about Grey. Once their week was up, would she see him again? Would she even want to?

Behind her she heard the lock on the bedroom door click. Turning, she saw Grey enter the bedroom with the tray. This time it was laden with French bread, cheese, pâté and wine.

Walking over to her he set the tray upon the bed, and Zoe stuck her finger into the pâté for a taste.

"It looks delicious," she said.

"So do you," Grey replied, watching her lick the pâté from her finger.

"Let me see." He motioned for her to turn and model in front of him.

"There isn't much to this," she answered, executing a slow turn. "And what there is, you can see right through."

"I know." Fitting his hand to the curve of her waist, skin on skin, he pulled her to him.

"But I'm chilly."

"I'll build a fire," he said, nibbling at her ear. "Mmm . . . you smell good." His mouth played at her neck, making shivery, sucking kisses that warmed her blood. For a fleeting moment she pictured the vampire in the book she'd been reading.

"What did you do while I was gone?" His mouth left her neck to bite the smooth roundness of her shoulder.

"I read and spent hours soaking in a bubble bath."

"Getting ready for me?" he asked, his hands moving to palm and squeeze the buttocks left bare by the thong bikini.

"No, staying warm. About that fire . . ."

"The fire, right." Releasing her, he indicated the tray of food. "Go ahead and eat while I build us a fire."

He took the matches from the whitewashed oak mantel and knelt to start a fire in the hearth. After using some pine for kindling, he added fruit wood once he had the fire going. The fire had lent a warm coziness to the room by the time they finished eating. The crackling apple wood gave off a sublime, incenselike aroma and bathed the room in a romantic glow.

Grey set the tray upon the floor beside the bed, then helped Zoe fluff the pillows behind them, so they could lie propped up and watch the flickering dance of the flames.

A bottle of wine had come and gone when he leaned over and kissed her. The kiss reminded her of her husband's first kiss; this kiss, like that one, was heartbreakingly sweet. She was momentarily lost in his embrace, wrapped in his need and desire until faint alarm bells sounded.

"Maybe we shouldn't do this," she said, pulling back, the blurry warmth of the wine making her emotional.

He studied her a moment, brushing whisper kisses on her lips before agreeing. "Okay, then let's lie here and talk."

"About what?"

He shrugged and fell back upon the pillows. "I don't know. Men...women, men and women...marriage...the dark side of our personalities...the allure of freedom. I want to know you, Zoe. Know your dreams, your desires. Know what kind of man you need."

"I'm not sure I know."

"You must have some ideas...."

The antique gold clock on the mantel ticked off the seconds as she considered his question.

"I want a man who's both a lover and a friend," she began. "A man I can trust, depend on...one whose feelings I understand. A man whose mind I'm able to read because...because we're that close."

"Do you think we could be friends?" he asked as a shifting log in the fireplace gave off a crackling shower of sparks.

She glanced at him, surprised by his question. "I thought you were a tough guy."

"And you don't like tough guys...at least, not that way."

"Not when their sense of masculinity needs to be constantly fed by male bonding. Not when that male bonding shuts me out."

"You're talking about..."

"That's right. There isn't much room in a marriage for a third party. It screws up the priorities. That's what ruined marriage for me. If I'd wanted to spend that much time alone, I would have stayed single or become a nun or something."

"Maybe your husband spent so much time at work because it was part of his job to establish close ties with his men. They had things in common to talk about...things they had to share with each other or go crazy."

"He could have talked to me."

"He might have wanted to, but didn't because he wanted to protect you more. To protect you from the world he saw as a cop. Or maybe he just got caught up in the male provider role ... some men do that. They get so caught up in making a living that they forget about the emotional input and caring so necessary to make a marriage work."

"The male provider role...that's been a hiding place for a lot of men. The truth is, maybe he just didn't care," she said, letting her insecurities surface. Why hadn't her husband wanted to talk to her, to share his life? Why had she had to leave him? Had leaving him been a mistake? Was there something there left to save, after all?

Grey shifted, turning and stroking her face ever so gently. "And you think I'm like that . . . ?"

She searched his face, his achingly seductive face, so arrogantly male . . . yet holding a quiet dignity.

"I don't know, do I?" she answered softly, looking away.

He fell back against the pillows. "You think this is all an act?"

"I think you've been keeping me at a pretty safe distance, that's what I think."

"What?"

"Maybe I'm vulnerable right now, but you are, too. You're hiding behind that cool image of yours."

"I think," he said, maneuvering to capture her wrists in a playful lunge, holding them prisoner at her side, "I think this is where I take my ribbons and go home. I'm the one who invented this game, remember." He gave her a sexy kiss, then levered himself back, grinning down at her. "It's not fair, you using it on me."

"The ribbons are on the dressing table," she said, imperiously dismissing his threat with a nod toward the colorful spill of satiny streamers. "And for your information, I've given up playing fair."

"I'll consider myself warned," he said.

"What?"

He lay back against the pillows. "I was just wondering why someone as beautiful as you stayed with the insensitive jerk as long as you did."

Her voice had a wistful note, she knew. "I believed in happy ever after, I guess."

"And now you don't."

She didn't answer. Instead she asked him a question. "What about you? What do you think about being married?"

He took her hand into his, bringing it to his lips for a lingering kiss. "I think whoever married you would

be a pretty lucky guy and a real jerk if he messed it up.
I wouldn't be so foolish as to take the chances he did."
His vow hung in the silent room. "What about you?"

"Me?"

"Yeah, you. Would you give marriage another try?"

"I don't know." Her long eyelashes swept her cheeks
as she practiced a coquettish look. "This clandestine
mistress business is pretty exciting." She trailed her
painted nails down his chest.

"You think so, do you?" His hand claimed hers, stilling it. Raising it to his lips, he sucked at her fingertips
with deliberate slowness. "What do you like about it?
The physical affection, the hugging and cuddling . . .
the romance?" He winked as he moved his hand to explore the contours of the daring thong bikini. "Or the
sexy presents?"

She grasped his wandering hand and laid it back
upon his bare chest with a pat. "All of the above—but
none of them are what I like the very most about it."

"Oh? And what is it that you like the very most about
being my mistress?"

"The fact that you find it so exciting," she whispered
into his ear, letting her lips linger to nibble at his lobe.
"You have especially sexy ears, you know."

He chuckled at her ploy. "Flattery will not distract me
from noticing your scheming . . . well, maybe a little . . ." he confessed when she flicked her tongue into
his ear. "But I told you, no analyzing me. I'm the only
one who is allowed to ask the questions."

"And I told you I don't play fair," she countered, chewing on his ear for emphasis. "So tell me, what do *you* find so exciting about having me for your mistress?"

"That's easy," he replied. Wickedness gleamed in his eyes and his smile had a wolfish slant. "I like locking you in."

She laughed out loud, caught off guard by his answer. "No kidding. I'd have to be blind not to notice you have a real penchant for doing that. Want to tell me why?"

"Not especially...." He made a real show of studying his fingernails.

"Come on...." She wriggled her fingers, "I'll tickle it out of you, so you may as well just go ahead and tell me."

"Okay, okay.... How about ... I'd do anything to keep you—" he smiled grandly "—a prisoner of my love?" he asked on what sounded like a hopeful note.

"I'm waiting, but not very patiently," she said, flexing her fingers for effect.

"You're venturing into exploring the dark side of my personality...."

"So let's explore, Doctor Sigmund. Inquiring minds want to know.... Why *do* you keep locking me in?"

He got up and walked over to the dressing table, where he toyed with the dresser set of hammered silver, running his hand over the mirror, comb and brush. He looked over the scattering of items on the dressing table and selected a box of dusting powder, carrying it back to the bed. After removing and discarding the cellophane wrapper from the box of dusting powder, he rejoined her on the bed, where he knelt before her. Lifting his eyebrows suggestively, he opened the box of dusting powder and brought it to his nose to sniff. The scent of spring rain drifted to her.

He turned his gaze from the box of powder to her. His eyes grew heavy, their pupils soft and wide.

"Undo the camisole top," he instructed hoarsely.

"If I do, will you answer my question?" she countered, hesitating.

"Yes."

Zoe began undoing the three tiny faux pearl buttons fastening the front of her delicate lace camisole. When the buttons came undone, she stretched forward . . . dipping her back to rest her weight upon her hands in a catlike pose, the sleek action causing her breasts to bob free of the constraint of the camisole, playing an erotic game of peekaboo with the bit of sheer fabric and lace.

Undulating onto her knees on the soft bed, Zoe played to the blue eyes watching her, getting high on the power of her femininity. She lifted her hands to her hair and mussed it sexily, all the while reveling in the effect she was having on Grey. Rotating her smooth shoulders, she shimmied out of the white camisole, letting it slip onto the bed.

Grey swallowed dryly. His eyes raked her pink and creamy prettiness as he dipped the soft powder puff into the round, deep box of scented dusting powder. Tapping the excess from the puff on the side of the box, he began smoothing the fragile puff over Zoe's tender skin, dabbing the scented powder across her collarbone, then across the lush tops of her breast.

The atmosphere in the room was still and intense. Finally he made a stab at returning to their abandoned conversation. "As I recall it, you were asking me why I had a penchant for locking you away in this room when I'm not with you?" He looked up from his handiwork and smiled at her stammered reply.

"I ... ah ... yes...."

The soft powder puff in his hand was a magic wand. It tickled and aroused at the same time. The sensations ... What Grey was doing made it almost impossible for her to concentrate on anything but his actions.

"Well," he began, redipping the powder puff, "I believe we're in agreement that you more or less ran away from your husband. That is what you told me over dinner in Paris, isn't it?"

She nodded, not looking at him.

"Let's just say I don't want a repeat performance. I wanted to make sure you would stay for a week. I didn't want to return to find you'd run out on me ... or your feelings."

"And that's why you keep locking me in?" she inquired, aware that her tone acknowledged the fact that more than mere physical restraint was involved.

"That's why," he said, dabbing her nose playfully with the powder puff, leaving a smudge of white powder. If she looked into a mirror, she knew she'd appear

Four Irresistible
Temptations
FREE!

PLUS A MYSTERY GIFT

Temptations offer you all the age-old passion and tenderness of romance, now experienced through very contemporary relationships.

And to introduce to you this powerful and highly charged series, we'll send you **four Temptation romances** absolutely **FREE** when you complete and return this card.

We're so confident that you'll enjoy Temptations that we'll also reserve a subscription to our Reader Service, for you; which means that you'll enjoy...

- **FOUR BRAND NEW NOVELS -** sent direct to you each month (before they're available in the shops).

- **FREE POSTAGE AND PACKING -** we pay all the extras.

- **FREE MONTHLY NEWSLETTER -** packed with special offers, competitions, authors news and much more...

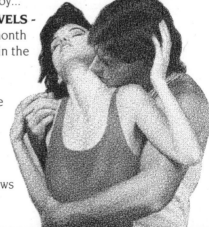

CLAIM THESE GIFTS OVERLEAF

Free Books Certificate

YES! Please send me **four FREE Temptations** together with my **FREE gifts.** Please also reserve a special Reader Service subscription for me. If I decide to subscribe, I will receive four Temptation romances each month for just £7.00 postage and packing free. If I decide not to subscribe I shall write to you within 10 days. The free books and gifts are mine to keep in any case. **I understood that I am under no obligation whatsoever.** I may cancel or suspend my subscription at any time simply by writing to you. I am over 18 years of age.

A Free Gift

Return this card now and we'll send you this cuddly Teddy Bear absolutely FREE together with...

A Mystery Gift

We all love mysteries, so as well as the FREE Teddy Bear there's an intriguing FREE gift specially for you.

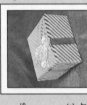

MS / MRS / MISS / MR

ADDRESS

SIGNATURE

_____7A2T

MILLS & BOON
FREEPOST
P.O. BOX 236
CROYDON
CR9 9EL

to have been baking. But she didn't have to look into a mirror to know she was cooking. The warm flush of her skin gave the fact away to Grey, as well.

"Okay, so you wanted to make sure I would stay for a week, as we agreed. But what about taking my clothes and leaving me with nothing, well, almost nothing, to wear?"

He chuckled. "If I didn't lock you in without something to wear, you'd find a way to escape. But without clothes you're less inclined to try." He leaned close, whispering naughty words about how she looked wearing next to nothing. His hands were busy, playing at her breasts, until a dull ache began to build at the juncture of her thighs above the white lace-topped stockings. Her eyelashes fluttered closed against her rosy cheeks.

When his hands stilled, her eyes opened once again, but her breathing was quick and shallow as she studied him consideringly.

"Suppose I locked you in a room with nothing to wear, kept you as a playmate . . ." she said, half threatening, half playful.

"I'd love it," he answered all too readily. "Wouldn't you?"

"It's . . . ah . . . the things are . . . I don't know."

"I think maybe you do like it, but you think you shouldn't."

"And I think you're avoiding my question," she said, sitting back on her heels.

He flashed her a guilty look. "Smart. Why do I have to be attracted to a smart woman?"

She laughed at his display of mock sorrow. "You're still avoiding the question."

"Okay, okay. The truth is, I want you naked or wearing something that compels you to think about your body, because I want . . ."

"Yes . . ."

"I want to free you . . ." he said on a sigh.

"Free me?" she repeated, looking at him with patent disbelief.

"Yes," he answered softly, then went on to explain. "I want to free you from all the shoulds, from your pre-conceived idea about what I want—what you want. I want us to explore who we are—to explore intimacy."

When she started to object he interrupted. "Yes, I know you were married, but just because you were married, it doesn't mean you've been intimate with a man."

"And you think we can't do this clothed and talking?"

He shrugged. "Later, perhaps. But not now. Now we would only remain strangers hiding behind our clothes, behind convention, behind the walls we've built. Walls every person builds to protect themselves—a wall that while keeping others out, keeps us imprisoned."

She heard the pain and loneliness behind his words and reached out to put her hands upon his in a gesture of comfort. "You're really serious about this, aren't you? Why? You don't strike me as the sort of man who's given to deep introspection. Why this need to search for more?"

He sighed again. "You're right, of course. I'm not introspective, not usually. Let's just say that one day it was brought home to me that everything I thought I knew, I didn't know at all. Growing up, I accepted things easily—the views of my parents, my teachers, employer, even just the culture of the times. It was okay, I suppose, when it worked. But then suddenly it didn't work anymore. So, like you, I've set out to find myself."

"And have you?"

"I think I'm on the right path," he said with a warm smile.

"And you think I can help you?"

He nodded. "I think we can help each other. Don't you?"

She sat looking at him thoughtfully until he spoke again.

"What? What are you thinking? Are you thinking about the marriage you left behind? Could you go back to the man you left, to the stable routine? Do you miss the security?"

His questioning became more impassioned. "Or could you put your lot in with a man like me?"

"A man like you?"

"A man like me. A man uncertain of what he wants in life, except for you. A man who makes no guarantees about his future, except that he wants you in it, helping him to shape it."

"Sometimes I do miss the security of my old life," Zoe said, answering honestly.

"Then you're sorry you left?"

"No. I had to leave. I'm sorry I hurt my husband. He didn't deserve to be hurt, not really. He was a good man who wanted to provide for me and keep me safe from the dangers of the work he did. But by keeping me safe, he locked me out of his life.

"And since I had no life of my own without him, I began disappearing before my own eyes. I knew it wouldn't be long before I started disappearing before his, and I couldn't bear it. I was a mirror he looked into, and I could no longer reflect what he wanted to see."

"Perhaps it was him. Perhaps he saw all too well. Maybe he knew he was losing you and didn't know how to stop it. Maybe that's why he hid from you, buried in his job. Because he didn't know how to hold on to you, he held on to the only thing he knew how to do, was good at."

"Maybe. Or maybe he'd just lost interest, grown past what I could give him."

"Did it occur to you that you might have grown past him? Past the macho life-style he demanded. He might not have known how to deal with the independent woman you were growing into and was threatened, but didn't know how to tell you. I don't want to make his mistakes, Zoe. I want everything between the two of us to be allowed. No secrets. No walls."

Zoe didn't say anything for a long while. "No secrets . . . no walls . . ." she agreed finally.

Her mood changed then as she grew playful. Winking at him, she took the powder puff from the box of loose powder, then teasingly dusted the insides of her thighs above the stockings. After returning the puff to its box, she used her hands to rub the smooth talc over the contours of her body. Her eyes drifted shut once again as she enjoyed the feel of her own touch, stroking ever so lightly. Slipping her fingertips beneath the thong bikini, she lowered it.

"Open your eyes."

Zoe answered Grey's command, to see his own eyes devouring her. "You were right," he said. "This clandestine mistress business is pretty exciting."

She smiled, reaching to pull up the bed linen, all of a sudden feeling like the modest maiden.

He leaned forward. "No," he said, taking the linen from her hands. "We agreed, remember. No secrets . . . no walls."

Brushing her lips with a kiss, he moved his mouth to whisper into her ear. "I want you to turn over," he said, reaching for the box of powder.

She hesitated, then did as he requested, watching him over her shoulder as he dipped the puff into the box to fill it with loose powder, then began dusting her bottom.

"What do you think you're doing?" she asked, laughing.

He put on his best French gendarme's accent and informed her, "A good detective, *chérie*, always dusts for prints."

She looked at him with wide eyes. "But Detective, there hasn't been a crime...."

He stopped and looked at her for a long moment. "Yet..." he said. "But I think you should know the suspense is killing me." Putting the powder puff back into the box, he rose from the bed.

"You're going to have to make a choice, you know," he said, opening the door and leaving her alone in the bedroom once again.

9

ZOE SAT NAKED in the middle of the rumpled bed, unable to sleep.

Grey's words haunted her.

He was right; she was going to have to make a choice. During the past six months she'd been busy exploring who she was. Busy becoming a modern independent woman. Busy enjoying her new friendship with Lauren-Claire.

Busy.

Purposely too busy to consider the future.

While she had proven to herself that she could survive on her own, she'd repressed the longing she had for loving. It had taken a stranger to open her up by daring her to come with him on a journey...a journey with no sexual boundaries.

He had shown her she'd been living a lie, hiding from herself. First in endless classes during her marriage, now in living from day to day in Paris, her life on hold.

Even these past few days with Grey had been busy ones.

They'd been pleasurable and exciting, but they were still only an idyll. A side trip away from making a decision about her life.

About what *she* wanted.

Not what the sweet, insensitive guy she'd married wanted. Not what the bold, mysterious stranger in the other room wanted. Not what Lauren-Claire thought she should want. Not even what the proliferation of women's magazines said she should politically and correctly want.

What *she* wanted.

Did Grey really think there was a chance she would return to her marriage? And what was Grey's fantasy? What did he want from her?

She sighed, her thoughts in turmoil. The room was cooling. She glanced at the fireplace; only a few glowing embers remained in the grate. The fire, like their lovemaking, had flamed and cooled. Throwing off the sheet she sat wrapped in, she went to the armoire. But it was empty, except for a few pairs of tissue-wrapped stockings and... Her eyes fell on the locked oblong box.

She gave in to temptation and carried the box back to bed with her, picking up a nail file on the way from the purse Grey had returned . . . passportless.

It took some doing, but she managed to pry open the box. She wasn't certain what to think when she saw its sole contents.

She was certain, however, of what had happened to the pair of silver handcuffs that had disappeared from the Porsche's rearview mirror.

Slamming the lid of the box shut, she set it away from her. The handcuffs were a sign of submission.

It occurred to her then that her relationship with Grey was not much different from the one she'd had with her husband. In both instances, she was not—had not been—the one in control.

It was time.

It was past time.

Tossing aside the sheet, she got up and went to the bedroom door. Turning the knob, she was surprised to find the door unlocked.

About to slip out, she stopped and went back to the bed. Opening the oblong box again, she stared down at the handcuffs consideringly. A sly smile crooked her lips as an idea took shape in her mind.

Not letting herself think about the wisdom of her actions, she picked up the pair of handcuffs. Pausing for a moment to get her bearings, she decided to investigate the bedroom adjoining hers on the left as the most likely place to find Grey. She had that feeling of being trapped in a Gothic novel again as she stealthily crept down the hall, lest a floorboard creak and give her away. She looked down at herself and amended her image to "modern Gothic novel"; she was a tad underdressed without the traditional, flowing white nightdress. She supposed she could have virginally wrapped a sheet around herself, but knowing her luck, she would probably have tripped on the trailing sheet and catapulted down the stairs, breaking something valuable besides her person along the way.

Inching along, she came to the door of the adjoining bedroom. As she reached for the knob, the handcuffs in her other hand jangled and she jumped. It was a definite drawback that birthday suits didn't have pockets, she thought, looking down at herself for someplace to put the handcuffs while she sneaked into what she hoped was Grey's room.

The handcuffs ended up in her mouth when she found the door unlocked but stuck, requiring both hands to shove it open discreetly. Trying not to think about the picture she made, she wrestled the door open without making any distinct creaking noises.

She put her eye to the narrow opening and peered into the room.

French doors stood open directly opposite, mocking her with their easy access from a balcony until she recalled her state of undress. A mahogany chair, slipcovered in white sheeting, was splashed with moonlight.

She could just make out the topiary container plantings, so popular in France, standing sentinel on the balcony. The window treatment at the balcony doors contained the same floral design as the walls. A large cylindrical basket of logs sat beside the fireplace, an exact match to the one in her bedroom. While a fire was laid out, it hadn't been lighted.

Her eyes turned farther to the left, only to be startled by the life-size, sculptured Roman torso near the draped bed. The lanky figure sprawled across the bed on his back was not headless, however.

She was sure of that, because he was snoring softly. Looking at the bedside table, she saw an open bottle of wine and half-full glass. She'd driven him to drink.

Good.

Thankful for the rug covering the sound of her feet as she crossed the room, Zoe watched Grey's face, carefully monitoring the sound of his snoring as she crept up to the head of the bed, where his head lay on a mound of floral-patterned pillows.

She took the handcuffs from her mouth and looked down at him. He was shirtless and shoeless, his disreputable jeans low on his lean hips, displaying his very flat belly, which moved almost imperceptibly with each breath he took as he continued to snore, sound asleep.

His arms were splayed over his head, conveniently near the brass headboard. All she had to do was be careful not to disturb his sleep. She didn't want to find herself on the receiving end of her brilliant idea.

Taking a deep breath, she eased herself onto the bed. He didn't stir. Good.

Reaching over his head, she very carefully slipped the handcuffs between one of the posts on the brass headboard and brought it back out, securing it in a U shape. Leaning back, she allowed herself to breathe again.

She looked down at him, his steady, light snoring assuring her he was still asleep. His dark hair had fallen across his forehead, and a shadow of night beard covered his square jaw. Moonlight played on his sharp cheekbones.

He didn't look innocent, even in sleep.

She had to be very, very careful.

Swallowing dryly, she lifted the arm nearest her and moved it to the handcuff dangling by the bedpost. He didn't move as she slipped the cuff around his wrist and locked it. She eased her hand away from his and let it fall back against the brass headboard.

Now the other wrist. She considered getting off the bed and going around to the other side, but decided getting on and off the bed once again was actually more likely to disturb his sleep.

Leaning across him, she held her breath, reaching for his free hand.

He moaned and she froze, her heart pounding in her ears.

"Mmm . . . you smell good . . ." he mumbled, nuzzling his face between her breasts. "I've missed you, baby. . . ."

Within moments he was snoring softly again.

How could a man do something so sexy and not wake up?

She was awake—really awake. And forcing herself to remain absolutely still. When she was convinced he was once again sleeping soundly, she made quick work of securing his other wrist in the handcuff. He was now her captive.

Backing off the bed, she stood upright, her knees nearly giving way. Steadying herself with one hand on the brass headboard, she finally allowed herself the release of a deep sigh.

He wasn't going to be pleased—not pleased at all. But that was okay, because now it was time for her to please herself.

Going to the armoire on the wall opposite the bed, Zoe selected one of Grey's shirts. It was sizes too big for her. The hem hit her at midthigh when she slipped into it, and the cuffs hung down way past her hands. She rolled up the sleeves as she left the bedroom, leaving the door open in case he woke up . . . though she imagined she would be able to hear him when he awoke.

In the kitchen she warmed some milk and raided a tin of tea biscuits, carrying them upstairs with her, then couldn't resist looking in on her handiwork one last time before retiring.

Though he was still fast asleep, his snoring had stopped. Somehow he'd managed to turn onto his side.

Smiling, she savored the moment. She had pulled off a pretty slick trick, if she did say so. Six months ago it would never have occurred to her to think up such a stunt, much less carry it out.

Shaking her head at what she'd done, she decided that maybe she'd just gone round the bend, after all. And Lauren-Claire wasn't here to tell her. A giggle escaped her lips at the thought of her friend. Whatever would Lauren-Claire think of what she'd gone and done?

She supposed it wasn't any worse than her friend's vow to lasso and hog-tie herself a cowboy. Maybe Lauren-Claire wouldn't be so shocked, after all. She'd most likely only be shocked by the fact that Zoe had had the nerve to do the handcuffing.

Come to think of it, she thought, taking a sip of warm milk, she was pretty shocked herself.

What *was* she doing? Maybe she had better rethink what she'd done. She had acted on impulse. She hadn't really thought it through. And that was what had gotten her in Paris in the first place.

"*This is interesting. . . .*"

The low, sleepy drawl stopped Zoe cold; warm milk splashed from her mug.

She faced the bed . . . and the music.

Except she was met with *le mauvais garçon* . . . Grey, grinning a classic, bad-boy grin.

"Shouldn't you be upset?" she asked, unnerved by his indolent acceptance . . . by that and the look in his eyes, the lazy assessment.

"You tell me."

Her hand shook as she went to set her mug and the tin of biscuits on a nearby desk, so she could turn on the light.

How was it he was still the one in control? she wondered, leaning back against the desk and looking at him through narrowed eyes. The fingers of her right hand rested on something cool made of metal—a pair of scissors.

It took all her skill to keep a poker face when she picked them up and walked toward him, brandishing them. "How fond are you of those jeans you're wearing?"

He laughed—a nervous laugh.

She stood over him, working her fingers in the scissors, so that the silent room echoed the snip, snip sound.

"I brought these jeans with me from America," he said.

"Really?"

"Uh-huh," he answered distractedly, his eyes on the snipping scissors.

"How come you haven't sold them? You can get a fortune here in France for American jeans," she said, tapping the scissors absently against her chin.

"These are my favorite jeans."

"What a shame...."

"You aren't planning on cutting them off, are you?"

"The jeans, you mean?"

"Yeah, the jeans.... What else would you be cutting off?" He looked a little pale.

"Depends on how you spell it. There's jeans and there's genes."

"You're kidding, right?"

She began toying with the scissors again, making that snipping sound. "Really, it would be no problem," she assured him. "I have noticed your jeans are a little, uh, snug."

"Please. If you just put the scissors down and ease the buttons open carefully when you take them off, I'll be fine, thank you."

"Oh, so polite. I like that."

"Okay, so put the scissors down...." he coaxed.

"No."

"No?"

"No."

"There's something else I should tell you, then."

"Really? What's that?"

"I'm not into pain."

Her smile was so pure, it frightened him when she cooed, "Trust me, this won't hurt a bit."

"Dear me," he said, closing his eyes.

They flew open again when he heard the scissors snip.

"No!"

"*Ye-es.*"

"Zoe, no! I mean it. I forbid you."

"Watch me." Holding her long hair out straight, she continued snipping, until all that remained was a gamine's cap of curls.

"Why did you do it?" he asked when she was done.

"Because *I* wanted to. Because tonight I want to be the one in control," she said, sitting down on the bed beside him. "Because tonight I want..." wanton desire lurked in her eyes as she cupped him intimately "..you."

"*Damn* woman."

"Mind your manners," she said, trailing her finger over his mouth.

"Does this mean I'm going to have to say please...?"

"Count on it."

"*Damn.*"

"What was it you said? Just slip the buttons open carefully?" she asked, doing just that.

"Who's going to undo your buttons?" he asked, blowing warm breath onto her neck as she worked, lifting the new, wispy curls at her nape. "Hey, you know what. I think I like your new haircut."

"So do I."

"Zoe?"

"Hmm..."

"Aren't you taking rather a long time to do that?"

"It's because you're not cooperating."

"Is that a fact? But what can I do to help, my hands being shackled and all?"

"Think cold shower."

"Ouch."

"They're all undone."

"I'd like to see that."

"What?"

"You coming all undone in my arms...except I guess that won't happen tonight." He clicked the handcuffs against the brass headboard.

"Stick around and find out," she said, tugging off his jeans.

"Cute."

"I think so," she said, touching his erection.

"You know you're going to get it."

"Uh-huh."

"That's not what I meant."

"Grey?"

"Yes?" he gasped.

"Shut up."

The moonlight provided just enough light for her to trace the planes and hollows of his sculptured body with her long nails.

She felt him shudder deliciously under her touch and bent to trail tiny kisses over each rib, ending at his navel.

Her teeth followed with biting nips at the base of him, making his legs grow rigid as he strained toward her, his hands unable to assist his quest.

"Lie still," she whispered, sliding her hands beneath his buttocks as she slowly licked the length of him until he was writhing, strangled moans escaping clenched teeth.

"Zoe . . ."

"Not just yet," she answered, controlling the pace of their lovemaking, high on the power.

She slid her body up the length of his, then straddled him. A sweetly scented breeze drifted in through the open French doors.

"What do you think?" she asked, toying with the buttons of the shirt she was wearing. "Should I take it off?"

"Definitely."

"I don't know," she teased. "I think I'll leave it on for a while."

His eyes flashed, and he made a sudden move that pinned her beneath him, where he held her with insistently urgent kisses, taking her breath away.

Moving his mouth to her ear, he whispered huskily, "Take it off, please baby, please."

"You'll have to let me up."

He rolled to one side, watching her as she slowly unbuttoned the shirt, then surprised him by pulling it over her head with one swift motion and dropping it to the floor.

He smiled as she crawled toward him, straddling him once again, her warmth settling against his belly. Leaning forward, she began teasing his face with her breasts, keeping them just out of reach of his clever tongue....

"Please..." he finally whispered huskily and she rewarded his politeness, introducing his mouth to first one and then the other—straining to stay in control as he went a little wild.

She pulled away from him finally, sitting up.

"Any special requests...?" she asked, still teasing, slowly rotating her hips as she sat astride him, so he could feel she wanted him.

He just stared hard at her, his eyes promising that if only his hands were free, she wouldn't be nearly so daring, so wicked, so bad.

"No?" she said, moving from him and off the bed. "In that case, I'll just take my milk and cookies and go to bed."

"Zoe..." The low growl was a command.

When she reached the doorway, she turned and looked back over her shoulder. "Was that an order I just heard in your voice?"

"No," he breathed, correctly judging her game.

"A request maybe, then...?"

He nodded. "A special request."

She turned and set the milk and cookies upon the desk.

"I can't hear you..." she said, playfully putting her hand to her ear.

"*S'il vous plaît*.... Please.... I want you."

"How bad do you want me?"

"As bad as you get."

Turning out the light with a low, sexy laugh, she proceeded to show him... to burn scorching, unforgettable images upon his memory, setting herself free.

"I've never made love to a woman like you," Grey said, smiling at her in wonderment later as they lay cuddling. After she had had her way with him, she'd wanted his arms around her. His eyes drifted closed as they lay sated, comforted and spent in the hazy afterglow of lovemaking.

Zoe sighed, content.

"Are you all right?" Grey asked, concerned.

She nodded, murmuring, "I'm fine, really fine."

"You are that," he agreed with a sleepy yawn, his hand patting her bottom in a sweet caress.

"And you're not so bad yourself," she added.

He laughed roughly. "That isn't what you said earlier, *chérie*."

Her remembering chuckle was wicked with naughty intonations. "But you're so good when you're bad...."

"I'll remind you of that when I can walk again. Right now, if I don't get some sleep, I won't be good for anything."

She lay beside him, her body still tingling with the imprint of his exquisite touch. He had staked his claim, freeing himself and reveling in her untapped sensuality. He'd been very vocal in his response—as had she. She smiled to herself; while their lovemaking had been white-hot, it had also been an exchange between equals.

She liked being equal. Liked it one hell of a lot.

While she had banished her insecurity, there were still some doubts and questions. She felt better than she had in a long time—even if her life had been turned upside down and inside out.

A GUST OF WIND rattled the balcony doors, waking Zoe from a deep sleep filled with erotic dreams of marble statues licked by flames. She opened her eyes to an unfamiliar room filled with bright sunlight. Blinking to adjust her eyes to the sudden brightness, she yawned, then stretched, sliding her hands into her hair.

Her hair!

It was short.

Images from the past evening filled her mind.

She looked over—to find Grey gone. In his place lay an envelope addressed to her.

Picking it up, she stared at the slash of her name on the pale envelope. Her heart hammered in premonition as she opened it. For a moment the words swam before her eyes—there was only one line of script, but it had the impact of a sucker punch.

Maybe this was a mistake.

Grey

What? She held her head, feeling a little fuzzy from the past night's wine and lack of sleep. What did this mean? Where was he? Had he gone completely?

"Grey," she called, getting up and pulling his shirt over her head.

There was no answer.

She went into her bedroom and crossed to the window, looking down on the entrance to the château. A sigh of relief escaped her lips. The Porsche was still there.

He'd just gone for a walk to think things over. She decided to draw a bath and think the situation through—she always did her best thinking in the bath. She'd use the time to bathe and get dressed, so they could talk when he returned from his walk.

She needed to collect her thoughts, too. But she found it hard to think of anything but Grey and their lovemaking—the incredible romance of the night they'd shared and the barriers she'd let down.

Would she ever really know the sensual, elegant creature she had been in the dark hours of the night? She was sure the husband she'd left would have been shocked by her wild abandon. A wild abandon that had strangely brought her a sense of control . . . power.

A sense of herself as a woman.

Letting go had been exhilarating beyond relief, and Grey had matched her, move for move. Had it been just the seductive quality of the night? Finding herself in a different situation had allowed her the freedom to express her sensual side, and for that she would always be grateful to Grey.

How did he feel about her?

It was more than sheer animal magnetism... though they had that in abundance. There had been more—something that spoke without words in the dark. Their attraction had been emotionally stimulating because of the acceptance they'd given each other. The daring exposure of their most secret selves had only enhanced the physical pleasure.

Her whole body ached with his lovemaking, her skin was alive as she moved the soapy sponge over it. Closing her eyes, the last several days drifted past in images...wisps of lingerie, white-lace-edged sheets, lazy laps in the pond, the knock of a croquet mallet hitting a ball, the firelight dancing over the hard contours of Grey's body, a whimsical carousel.

Could their love and desire only survive when they retreated from the world? What would they be to each other in the revealing light of day?

She poured a luxurious amount of shampoo into the palm of her hand and began soothing it through her short cap of curls.

Was she being scandalously self-indulgent? Perhaps. But she'd settled for less, compromised her needs, only to find the deal came with a heavy price.

Maybe it wasn't fair to blame her husband; she truly knew his heart had been in the right place. There had been a lot right with her marriage. Her husband had taken his vows seriously, wanting to protect and honor her.... There hadn't been other women. But she'd had to compete against his job. He hadn't meant to make her unhappy. He'd only neglected to make her happy... or to allow her to make herself happy.

One thing was certain. Grey had rocked her world.

She knew there was no perfect person, just as there was no perfect relationship. The goal of a relationship should be for each to help the other to be the best person he or she could be.

She was happy, but confused about her feelings when she left the bath to dress.

Wrapping herself in a plush bath towel, droplets of water still on her shoulders, she went into Grey's bedroom to retrieve the mug and tin of biscuits to return them to the kitchen. She would see what she could scrounge up to fix him for breakfast. Surely there would be enough to make omelets. He should be back soon from his walk, and the exercise would have made him hungry.

As she was turning to leave the bedroom, a flutter of filmy plastic caught her eye in the armoire. She went to investigate and found her hunch had been right. Grey was keeping her dry cleaning there. Now she had something to wear.

Something made her pause and look back at the armoire. Going back to it, she saw what had troubled her. It was empty of Grey's clothes. She glanced around the room. Nothing of his remained. No toiletries, no tennis shoes or cowboy boots. Nothing.

"Grey?" she called, a sinking feeling settling in her empty stomach.

Leaving the bedroom, she hurried down the stairs.

In the hall was the confirmation of what she feared. Moving aside the car keys and money laid on top her passport, she picked up the note.

The few scribbled lines on the paper hit her hard.

He hadn't gone for a walk to think about them.

He'd left her.

The coward.

10

ZOE REREAD THE NOTE when her eyes had cleared from the first shock of reading what it said. The château was rented for three more days, if she wanted to stay on. When she was ready, she could drive the Porsche back to Paris and leave it parked outside the loft, where he would have it picked up.

He was confused, needed time to think and was going to hitchhike to the South of France.

She tapped the note against her hand. Had she been so very wrong about what they had shared during the past few days?

No. She was good for him. Why, he hadn't even smoked one cigarette since they'd arrived . . . not even after last night. She had turned an arrogant, aloof man into a man who smiled and laughed out loud.

Her decision was instantaneous.

She was going after him. She'd have to hurry dressing and gathering everything up if she hoped to catch up to him. She'd already lost precious time dawdling in the bath in a haze of romantic bliss.

Whom was she kidding? she admonished herself as she took the stairs two at a time. With a destination as vague as the South of France she was going to need nothing short of a miracle to find him.

In less than ten minutes she was ready. Rushing downstairs, she caught sight of herself in a mirror and realized she now looked French with her short haircut.

Grabbing the keys to the Porsche, she pulled the door shut behind her. As she hurried down the lavender-lined path, she began sneezing, remembering the night she'd arrived at the château asleep in Grey's arms . . . Sleeping Beauty, awaiting the prince's kiss to wake her from her slumber.

Grey's kisses had certainly done that, weaving some sort of enchantment over her. Oddly she was in high spirits despite the situation. She possessed a strength and confidence she couldn't have imagined before this idyll.

Reaching the Porsche, she climbed inside, glancing nervously at the loaded cockpit. Taking a deep, steadying breath, she grasped the steering wheel and inserted the key into the ignition, feeling the power of the low sports car purr to life beneath her hands.

"Take me to your owner," she pleaded, putting the car into gear, wincing at the stripping sound, tires spewing gravel as she headed south in search of Grey.

Finding him was of the utmost importance, though she wasn't sure exactly why—or what she planned after. But she vowed she would find him.

How hard could it be in a country no larger than Texas? That made her think of Lauren-Claire and wonder how she was doing in Texas in her search for a cowboy or two.

A few kilometers down the snaking country road, she passed a weathered sign directing her to a picturesque village. *Why, Zoe, I don't believe we're in Kansas anymore!*

She paid little heed to the speedometer as the sleepy medieval villages whizzed past. There wasn't a lot of traffic on the road. Hadn't she read somewhere in the travel literature that in the countryside of France, the clang of cowbells signaled rush hour?

Maybe she could reach Grey before someone offered him a ride. A bicyclist appeared up ahead and waved as she passed by. Misty clouds shrouded the mountains dotting the horizon. The Porsche was eating up the miles when she came up on a rusting *camionnette* driven by a farmer.

It took all her willpower not to blast her horn as he lurched along in front of her, slowing down her chase. She did, however, use up her knowledge of Anglo-Saxon swear words by the time they came to one of the wide spots in the road where she could pass.

Glancing down at the fuel gauge, she saw she needed gas. At the gas station she pulled over to refuel. After gassing up from one of the old-fashioned green and white pumps, she pulled out her credit card.

"Hi, you're an American, aren't you?" the attendant asked, writing up the sale.

"You speak English," Zoe said in surprise.

"My mom's American. She came over one summer during school vacation and met my dad and as they say, 'That was all she wrote.'"

Zoe nodded. It appeared that France was a popular place to get lost and find yourself.

"Are you on vacation?"

"An extended one. I've been living in Paris for the past six months."

She returned the charge slip to him and he tore off her copy, returning it to her with a smile. "Funny, you're my second American today."

Zoe looked up from putting the charge slip and her card into her wallet. "Really? When was this?"

The attendant shrugged. "I don't know. Maybe fifteen minutes ago, I guess. The guy came in to get a soda and a pack of cigarettes."

Hurrying to her car, Zoe drove in the direction the attendant said the American was heading. In her mad rush to find him, she almost missed him. She slammed on the brakes, bringing the Porsche to a screeching halt.

"Nice piece of driving there," he said when she climbed out of the car. He threw down the cigarette and crushed it out.

He stood there with an air of casual confidence, looking devastatingly handsome.

"You forgot something," she said, reaching into the car. Straightening, she walked toward him with the pair of silver handcuffs dangling from her finger.

His eyes darkened and flashed with memory. "You don't really think I'll ever be able to forget these, now do you?"

She swallowed, gulping air.

"Is that all . . . ?" he asked, training his full attention on her, looking as if he were about to move on, if it was.

"No," she said softly. "You forgot something else."

"What's that?"

"Me."

"Oh, I didn't forget you. You came along every step of the way, believe me."

"Then let's talk about it. Come on, I'll give you a ride back."

"Uh-uh."

She had already turned, expecting him to follow. His refusal stopped her. She turned back to face him, a question on her lips.

He shrugged, stuffing his fingertips into the front pockets of his jeans and rocking back on the heels of his cowboy boots. "I don't think we can go back . . . only forward."

"What are you saying?"

"Come along with me to the South of France," he offered, "I've only got two more days till I have to fly back to the States. I've got a flight booked out of Nice."

"What am I supposed to do when you leave?"

"I thought that's what we'd talk about. . . ."

She hadn't been prepared for the invitation. This was the part she had no plan for. She really needed to get better at making plans.

"Look Zoe, I'm confused about what we are to each other. I didn't know we were going to . . . to explode together like we did. . . . Maybe if we spend the little time we have left together in the real world, we'll find some answers."

"I . . ."

"I'm sorry about leaving," he apologized softly.

"Why did you leave?"

"Why did you leave your husband?"

"This is different."

"Is it? Or is leaving what we do when we're afraid of losing someone . . . ourselves, even?"

It was dangerous to want someone so badly, she thought, looking at him and accepting his offer, walking around to take the passenger seat in the Porsche. She wondered when she watched him stow his jacket and duffel if there was some symbolism in the fact that Grey was once again in the driver's seat.

It began to drizzle shortly after they were underway, and she was glad to have him navigate the hills, curves and switchbacks that were so disorienting that sometimes she couldn't tell if another car was approaching or heading in the same direction.

Even Grey made a miscalculation, uttering a vehement epithet when he hit a pothole big enough to accommodate a wild turkey.

They drove in silence, exploring their own thoughts as they sped through the Auvergne region with its pretty lakes. Stopping only for lunch, they shared some of the local cheese, as well as a hearty loaf of bread and bottle of wine.

Zoe succumbed to sleep as the Porsche purred along under Grey's capable hands when they got underway again. She didn't wake to notice as they drove on through the Rhône Valley past castles, churches and hillsides dotted with vineyards, as the air took on the beginnings of Mediterranean warmth. The shadows of evening were starting to fall when they entered Provence.

WRAPPED IN A SHEET, Zoe stood on the little terrace outside their room. The butter-yellow sunlight greeted her, welcoming her to the intoxicating sensuality that was the South of France...Provence, the home of Paul Cézanne.

She could hear Grey singing an old Motown favorite in the shower.

She smiled at the happiness in his voice. The shower stopped and moments later Grey came out. He undid the towel that was tied at his hip and used it to dry his hair.

Zoe thought the intoxicating sensuality that was Grey could give the South of France a run for its money.

"Where exactly are we?" she asked finally, when he had finished drying his hair and tossed the towel aside.

He came to stand beside her and looked out over the well-tended garden filled with a profusion of lavender flowers.

"We're in Fontvieille, at an eighteenth-century olive mill that has been turned into an intimate inn," he answered.

"It's an improvement," she said.

"How's that?"

"Well, I still have my clothes, and you didn't lock me in."

"That's because we aren't staying. We're leaving after breakfast. And where you're going, you won't be needing much in the way of clothes, *chérie*."

"And where is that?"

"The beach at Cannes," he said with a sexy wink as he trailed his fingertips over the nape of her neck. "You'll feel absolutely dowdy if you don't throw inhibition to the wind and go topless...."

"Not me," she promised.

"Coward," he challenged. "Come on, get dressed. You can borrow one of my shirts if you like. We'll have some breakfast and then head on out to—" he waggled his eyebrows lasciviously "—hit the topless beaches of Cannes."

When she didn't move, he pulled her sheet away and playfully swatted her bottom. "Hurry, I'll order breakfast while you shower and dress," he said, tugging on a pair of jeans. He'd either run out of underwear or had given it up altogether.

No, the South of France was not a place she was going to be at her best, when it came to decision making. Uttering a resigned sigh, she gathered up her things and headed for the shower.

They ate what had to be the best breakfast in Provence under a parasol on the terrace. The scent of pine trees lingered in the air as they looked out over the olive groves and cypress trees. Their leisurely meal was sweet and unhurried as they enjoyed the sunny golden climate.

By meal's end they had soaked up a certain joie de vivre that set the mood as they headed for Cannes, armed with information from their genial hosts.

CANNES, like Saint-Tropez, was the forbidden fruit of the Côte d'Azur.

It defined the word hot.... The holiday atmosphere was a punch-drunk Mecca of pleasure for the senses. Cannes was a glamour capital, the beautiful and the tacky flourished alongside each other, Zoe noticed as they strolled hand in hand along the rue Meynadier, shopping for bathing suits and suntan oil.

"I've got to make a call," Grey said when they had everything they needed. Using a phone card, he made the call at a public phone.

"Work or pleasure?" Zoe asked when he rejoined her.

He picked up a fringed scarf she'd been looking at and handed it to the salesclerk. "Work."

Zoe waited while the clerk rang up the sale, but Grey didn't elaborate. "You're not going to tell me about it, are you?" she asked when they left the shop.

"This is vacation.... I don't want to talk or even think about work."

"What do you want?" she asked as they walked past several palatial hotels lining the famous boulevard, the smell of the sea air luring them to frolic on the beach. Nearby were beautiful pine-covered hills and steep mountains, but the beach was unfair competition on such a sublimely sunny day.

"Let's go back to the hotel and change into our swimsuits," he suggested. "And then I want to forget all about work. All I want is to soak up the pleasures of summer and sea, gaze up at the luminous blue sky while lying on the white sandy beach."

"That sounds wonderful," she agreed. "But is there life after vacation?"

"For us, you mean? Yes. Well, that is the question, isn't it?" he asked as they entered the elevator to go up to their room. Once there, he pulled his swimsuit from a shopping bag and tossed her a pair of forties-style second-skin shorts.

She supposed she should be grateful he hadn't picked out a thong bikini, knowing his penchants. "The top, too," she said, holding out her hand.

"I don't think there is one," he said, grinning wickedly as he gazed into the tissue-stuffed bag.

"Grey. . ." she threatened.

"Okay, okay. Here it is," he answered, pulling it from the bag and tossing it to her.

They changed and headed to the beach; he with his jeans over his suit and she wearing the striped, skintight briefs that hit just below her belly button and skimmed her buns. On top was a matching push-up bra. The outfit was the latest fashion and threatened to replace the bikini.

"Let's go to a beach where it isn't too crowded, so we can talk. . . ." He tapped her nose playfully and trailed his finger along her cleavage. "And you can take off your top."

"I told you. . . ." She swatted his hand away from the playground.

"Yeah, yeah."

"You're not listening."

"I thought you wanted me to talk."

"I give in," she said as she headed out.

"Admirable quality in a woman, that," he said, stealing a kiss.

When they arrived at the discreet and slightly out-of-the-way beach, she was surprised to find no sand on its long wooden jetty, no beach balls, no noise, no kids.

"I think I love you, lie down," Grey said, continuing to torment her.

"You're impossible, you know that."

"No, just difficult," he disagreed, pulling her down beside him after shucking out of his jeans.

Lying lazily beside him, she watched sailboards glide by, riding the Mediterranean breezes. This, then, was the Côte d'Azur of her favorite F. Scott Fitzgerald book, she thought dreamily, taking note of the mix of cobalt, turquoise and green in the water.

Were she and Grey fated to end unhappily like Scott and Zelda?

Not looking at Grey, she asked, "What's important to you in a relationship?"

"I don't know.... Having someone to cheer me when I'm down, someone to encourage me. Maybe someone to love me unconditionally."

"You don't want a lover, you want a mother."

"Oh, and what do you want...? Someone to take care of you, freedom *and* commitment.... Is that it?"

"Isn't there some compromise, some place in the middle where we might meet?"

"Perhaps. What made you unhappy in your marriage?"

"Sex."

"What, not enough or too much?"

"It had nothing to do with the quantity, except for the fact that he was always the one to initiate it. It had more to do with the level of our sex life. It was okay, but it stayed in a sort of low gear. It didn't grow more intimate."

"Maybe intimacy is easier, less dangerous with a stranger. Did you ever show your husband how turned-on you were by any of his advances? I'm aroused by an openly responsive woman, but if my wife weren't into sexual self-expression, I might be hesitant to risk..."

"What?"

"Her opinion of me. I'd never want to be less than her hero.

"I seem to have lost complete control of this whole situation somewhere along the line," he said, sitting up and frowning as he looked at her. He was pensive for a moment, then his scowl was replaced by the familiar wicked grin. "The least you could do is put some suntan oil on me...."

"Sure," she agreed absently, her attention caught by a sun worshiper in Day-Glo orange shorts and matching zinc oxide on his nose; not that unusual a sight, except for the fact that he was a senior citizen. He waved as he jogged past.

Turning onto his back, Grey luxuriated in the feel of Zoe's hands massaging in the suntan oil; his skin felt warm and alive to her touch. He began to relax, the kinks of the long hours of driving melting away. His eyes closed.

Zoe's thoughts drifted over the days and nights they'd shared. The images were a montage of his hands, his mouth, his body beneath...above her, the sound of his laughter, and his groans of passion.

"You can turn over now...."

He looked over his shoulder at her, clearly confused. He blinked again, obviously having been on the same sort of mind trip she had—the physical evidence was blatantly obvious.

"I must be pretty good with my hands, huh?" she teased, pouring a pool of suntan oil into the palm of her hand and smoothing it over his chest and shoulders.

"You're enjoying this a little too much. It feels more like revenge than restitution," he said, grabbing her hand and stilling it. "My turn."

She had an image in her mind of him as a big old orange cat, pretending to doze outside a mouse hole, just waiting to pounce. The trouble was he had such lovely cheese to bait her with, she thought, giving in to the look of sweet desire in his eyes and his very obvious yen for her...er...soul.

Turning onto her back, she waited for...anticipated...desired his touch. Her body had gotten used to the regular attention, the feel of skin on skin.

"You will be a gentleman, won't you?"

"Trust me."

Why had that sounded like a taunt? she wondered.

His fingers, long and expert, started at the nape of her neck, his thumbs rubbing tiny circles. Her willpower was gone by the time he got to her shoulders.

How was she going to survive without this?

What was she going to do? What about her husband? Did her marriage deserve a second chance? Or did she prefer this sexy-as-sin stranger who lived by his passions?

"What are you plotting, sweet witch?" he whispered, leaning forward to nuzzle her ear.

My downfall, she thought in silent answer.

His hands continued their seductive massage, sliding over her back in sensuous arcs.

"Wait a minute! You've undone my top!" she said, levering herself up to face him, her hand holding the push-up bra in place.

"Yep."

"What happened to 'trust me'?" she demanded, trying hard not to laugh.

He didn't look the least bit repentant. Instead, he coaxed her further. "Come on, Zoe, live a little. Take it off."

She looked at him, his fierce gaze urging her on.

"I dare you."

She looked around them. The scattering of sun worshipers didn't seem to be paying any attention to them. "Say I do."

"I do. I did. I will."

"No, silly. I mean if I take it off, you agree to pay off on the dare."

"What? You want me to take off my trunks?" he asked, hooking his thumbs into them.

"Wait. No," she said, stopping him, pretty sure he was teasing her.

"What, then?" he asked suspiciously, his eyes narrowing as if trying to read her mind.

"I'll think of something," she promised him.

"I'm not sure I like the sound of that," he hedged. "Sounds like a sucker play to me."

"Hey, it's your game." She shrugged her shoulders, stringing him along, knowing she was going to reel him in regardless.

"I'm waiting," she said.

"Aw hell, all right. Though I have a feeling I'm going to regret the payoff."

She just smiled.

"Yeah, I lost complete control of the whole situation somewhere along the way," he muttered.

She laughed.

"I'm waiting," he said.

She dropped her top, feeling bold . . . adventurous and . . . weird to let everyone see her half-naked. She couldn't believe she'd actually done it, but from the

moment she did, she felt a thrill of freedom...
liberation... of being at one with the sea and sky.

Looking sexy and wicked, he began rubbing his
hands, then twining his fingers together and turning his
hands inside out.

"What do you think you're doing?" she asked,
laughing nervously.

"Just limbering up," he said, reaching for the bottle
of suntan oil. "After all, we can't have you burning such
tender skin, can we?"

"No," she agreed, barely able to speak as she watched
him pour a pool of oil into the palm of his hand.

Once again he slid his hands together and then he
molded the satiny fullness of her, but instead of watching what he was doing, he watched her eyes. Watched
what his touch did to her... watched her come apart
in his hands.

And then he coaxed her into doing what she'd secretly wanted to do since arriving at the beach...coaxed
her into running topless along it and splashing into the
surf.

11

THE FOLLOWING MORNING the sound of gently falling
rain woke them. When they finally got up, Grey showered first, then went down to the hotel boutique to buy
her something to wear in the rain. He found a metallic
trench coat that she could wear as a dress with low-
heeled pumps.

It was a perfect day for browsing the antique shops.
Grey insisted on buying her an antique stickpin and she
bought him something from the store's collection of fin
de siècle cuff links—just about maxing out her credit
card.

As they shared a marron glacé Italian ice she wondered if the gifts would become treasured mementos of
their early days together or sad remembrances of what
might have been.

Grey was right.

She did have a choice to make. But she wouldn't
think . . . couldn't think of it on their last day together.
It wasn't a decision to be entered into capriciously. She
had to face the fact that when they parted tomorrow,
it might be for ever. But, like Scarlett, she preferred to
think about that tomorrow.

And he'd never told her he loved her.

They took the old-fashioned ferry to the Îles de Lerins, where they explored the two small, lush islands that lay off the coast. Fort-Sainte-Marguerite was the site of a seventeenth-century fortress where the Man in the Iron Mask had been imprisoned. On Saint-Honorat they explored the medieval monastery now occupied by Cistercian monks.

When they returned to Cannes, she was still in an exploring mood and wanted to visit the museum and galleries. After stopping at a pastry shop to try its buttery *petits sablés* cookies, they headed in search of a museum.

Zoe was delighted by the last museum. They'd stumbled upon a photo exhibition. There were over two hundred works assembled for display.

"You really like this, don't you?" Grey mused as they strolled through the rooms with their impressive collections.

"It's like an addiction," she admitted. "I like the photography and painting, as well. What I really want to do is figure out a way to use the two of them together, in collages or something," she said as they left a group of fashion photographs and entered another room, showing the work of an artist with a weakness for forests.

A grouping of Hollywood portraits caught Grey's attention but it was the display of a variety of interpretations of urban streets that held his interest the most.

The museum was nearly deserted, being closing time, when they came to the last room. Here there were evocative photographs of lovers taken by a photographer whose work was extremely sensual in style. After studying the images, Grey and Zoe looked at each other.

Walking over to a window splashed with rain, she turned her back to the wall and crooked her finger at him.

"What?" he asked, tilting his head and glancing into the hallway to see if anyone was coming.

She continued to crook her finger, her eyes soft and dewy and began unknotting the belt of her metallic trench coat.

Glancing out the doorway one last time, he went across the room to her.

"What are you doing?"

She smiled.

"No. Uh-uh. No way, Zoe."

Footsteps sounded in the hall and a couple of teenage girls entered the room to begin browsing through the display.

"See," Grey admonished her, reknotting her belt.

The girls suddenly realized they were late for an assignation on the beach and didn't finish looking at the photographs, only giving Grey and Zoe a cursory glance as they left the room.

Zoe looked at Grey and smiled again, her hands going back to the belt of her trench coat.

"Will you quit that," he said, swatting them away.

"But you promised," Zoe complained with a pout, her eyes dancing, sort of glassy and hot.

"I did no such thing. Someone could walk in again."

"I want to."

"Zoe, no."

"You agreed."

"When? What are you talking about?"

"The beach yesterday, my taking my top off, you do remember that, don't you?"

He grinned, all wolf. "Yeah, I remember."

"Then you must also remember you owe me a pay-off." She'd unknotted the belt, her hands were working on the buttons.

"Zoe, we'll be caught and thrown in the Tower," Grey said, walking over to check the doorway yet again. From where he was standing, he could see a guard talking to a tourist near the front doors.

"That's England, we're in France," she said, finished with the buttons.

Grey turned back to her. "Okay, dungeons, then. Is that any better?"

"You know what?" she said, flashing that secret little smile again.

"What?"

"You talk too much," she answered, opening the trench coat.

"Stop that!" he said, motioning to her with his hands.

"Are you saying that you're reneging on your promise?" she asked as he watched her spellbound.

"No, but could we talk about this somewhere else?" He was trying to gauge how long the guard and tourist would continue talking.

"Gr-rey..."

He turned his attention back to her. Zoe had slipped off her white lace bra. She was naked except for the filmy white garter belt and pale stockings...and the white satin and lace thong bikini that was etched forever on his mind.

"What the hell...?" he swore, giving in.

"Where did you ever get such an idea?" he asked, his hands cupping her firm breasts, massaging them as his lips urgently kissed a path down her slender neck, his actions pressing her against the wall. He was pulsing and hard.

"From Alexia," she whispered.

"Alexia...who's Alexia?" he mumbled, his mouth replacing his hands and skimming and teasing her nipples into tingling, anxious pleasure, dampening her. He strained to attune his ears to the hallway, past the pounding of his heart.

"I met her in the one and only aerobics class I took. In our last class together, I told her I was going to take some art classes, and she divulged something that had happened between her husband Crew and herself when they first met. He followed her to a gala opening of an exhibit at the art museum one rainy night and cornered her in an alcove, where they almost did it."

"I think the key word here is *almost*," Grey said, coming up for air.

"You want to stop…?" she whispered, licking her lips temptingly.

He listened again for the sound of approaching footsteps. Nothing. Hopefully the guard was still with the tourist and no one else had entered the museum.

"I can't," he said, breathing heavily, his mouth as dry as cotton from the rush of fear of discovery and the excitement of it.

"Me neither," she said, pulling his lips back down to hers.

"Help me out of these," she whispered, bringing his hands to her thong bikini.

His tongue brushed past her teeth to explore the sweetness of her mouth in a wild, damp, eating kiss and then he leaned forward to slip the scrap of lacy panty down her long legs.

She braced her hands on his wide shoulders and stepped out of them.

Rising with them in his hands, he was momentarily at a loss and hastily stuffed them into the pocket of his bomber jacket. "Is it hot in here?" he asked, feeling as if he was burning up with fever.

"I wouldn't know," she said with a giggle. "I'm practically naked." She shifted one long, stocking-clad leg provocatively.

"Don't tease me," Grey warned, snapping her garter playfully on her thigh, noting the flush of her skin and the fine sheen of perspiration on her lightly tanned breasts.

Her lips were swollen, inviting.

Taking a deep, tremulous breath, he unsnapped, then unzipped his jeans, wincing at the sound they made.

Sliding his hand beneath her open coat, he pulled her to him, thrusting into her waiting smoothness. She wrapped her arms around him and hid her naked breasts against his chest. On an oath of desire, he moved his hands to her buttocks, pulling her to meet his urgent thrusts.

Moaning, she wound her hands into his hair, clenching and unclenching her fingers, giving herself up to his passionate lead.

They had only a vague notion of their surroundings, their range of vision had narrowed so much that they were virtually blind at the moment of exquisite, peaking pleasure, when their senses exploded.

"Bonjour, monsieur." Zoe sighed.

"Sweet witch," Grey groaned softly, breathlessly and then they were enveloped in a still and peaceful calm filled only with the sounds of their labored breathing.

"Is anybody still back here? It's closing time."

Muscles that had been agreeably slack only seconds before jumped at the approaching footsteps of the forgotten guard.

"Damn!" Grey whispered. "He's coming all the way back."

Zoe's nimble fingers closed her metallic trench coat, knotting the belt, while Grey hastily zipped and snapped his jeans, only a heartbeat before the old guard poked his head around the corner.

"Uh…" Grey's voice cracked. "We were uh…just…"

"Leaving," Zoe supplied, grabbing his hand.

"Yes, that's right, we're finished...er, that is...well, goodbye, then."

"Good day to you, too," the guard said with a friendly wave as they more or less bolted.

Once they were back outside on the street, they leaned back against the museum and broke up in laughter.

"Do you realize we were almost caught?" Grey said, his eyes bright and accusing.

"I think—" Zoe said, regaining her composure, raking her nail down the side of his jaw, "—the key word here is *almost*."

"You are a sweet witch," he said, pulling her into his arms. "An enchantress. What am I going to do with you?"

"Isn't it more like what are you going to do without me?" she asked, kissing him senseless.

12

THEY ATE IN THE CAR on the drive from Cannes to Monaco, later that evening.

"Mmm . . . this is so good."

Grey shook his head, glancing at Zoe. "I can't believe you came to Cannes, where they have some of the best food in France . . . some of the best food in the world, and you chose to eat this instead."

Zoe smiled at him. "But this is great French food . . . *le French fries, le burger* and *le shake*," she insisted.

"I give in," he said, rolling his eyes, then biting into the juicy hamburger she held to his lips.

"Admirable quality in a man, that," she teased, then made a slurping noise as her shake bottomed out. Her eyes feasted on a beautiful clump of wild irises beside the road as they continued their journey toward Monaco and the casino in Monte Carlo.

"Are you sure this is a good idea? What time is your flight out of Nice International in the morning, anyway?"

"I thought we could stay up all night. I can sleep on the plane."

"What about me?"

"You could come home with me. . . ."

When she didn't answer, he supplied another suggestion. "I'll have the Porsche picked up in Nice and get you a rail pass so you can sleep on the train to Paris."

"You have the answer to everything, don't you?" she said, feeding him the rest of her fries.

Picking up his shake, he polished it off, then looked at her again. "No. There are some questions only you have the answer to."

He was wrong, she thought, studying his profile. She didn't have the answer, either.

The closer they got to Monaco, the more luxury cars she spotted. Any way she looked at her situation, she was way out of her element.

When they reached the border of the small principality, discreet cameras recorded the license plates on the Porsche before they entered the craggy coastal hills of Monaco, locked against the Mediterranean Sea.

Getting his bearings, Grey headed uphill to Monte Carlo after consulting the map, tackling the principality's famous hairpin turns with zest.

"Isn't Monte Carlo lovely?" Zoe said, noting that every inch was either under development or neatly manicured with formal plantings.

"That it is," he agreed, parking the Porsche when they arrived at their destination.

After securing them a private suite, he led her to it. "You know, if your stomach had held out, we could have had lobster at Rampoldi," he said, opening the door. "I'd planned for us to have a romantic dinner there for our last night together before I left."

Zoe shrugged. "Can I help it if Lauren-Claire's gotten me hooked on American junk food again?"

"Is that all you miss about the States?"

"No," she answered, taking a pair of black taffeta evening pants, sequined black lace bustier and matching satin and lace pumps from her shopping bag.

"Then you could be happy living there again?" he asked, hanging a rumpled dark suit in the bathroom and turning on a hot shower to dewrinkle it.

"I need to use the shower," she said when he closed the bathroom door.

He remained in front of the door, blocking her way. "You didn't answer my question."

"Where I live doesn't make me happy or unhappy, I've discovered. I do that."

"All by yourself..." he said, leaning against the door with his shoulder, forearms crossed.

"With a little help from my friends," she conceded with a shrug.

"Friends..."

"Like Lauren-Claire. It was a stroke of luck meeting her in Paris. She's fun and carefree. Her exuberance keeps me from being too narrow in my perspective. Without her I'd probably work all the time."

"You'd get caught up in your art like your husband got caught up with being a cop..." he said, playing devil's advocate.

"Touché."

"And this Alexia person..."

"She's more like me, driven to improve herself. At least she was until she married Crew."

"The guy who taught her the trick about . . . ah . . . taking the time to really . . . er . . . appreciate museums, the way you taught me."

She nodded.

"Heck of a guy," he said, his eyes dancing.

"The shower . . . before all the hot water's gone," she reminded him.

"Sure," he agreed magnanimously, moving aside so she could go in.

As she stood in the shower with the water streaming over her, she thought back over the past week and how she'd felt being Grey's mistress. It had been an exciting and educative experience. They had both explored their sexual boundaries. She certainly hadn't found him wanting as a lover.

She had been selfish and so had he, but in a giving way. Zoe knew that until she was sure of who she was, she wouldn't be able to give herself completely to another. She knew now that the failure of her marriage was partly her fault. She'd expected her husband to fix everything. Sure, she'd gone to classes to try to improve herself, but it had really been her way of running away.

She'd been inventing a new person. Perhaps her husband wasn't so much to blame; he'd been confused. They had both been so very young. Too young, she realized now. He hadn't known enough not to get lost in his job, and she hadn't known enough to stop him.

And to be honest, she had chosen the easy way out instead of deciding to stay and fight for their marriage—for him.

Over the past week she'd found that while she liked being out of control, she also needed some structure in her life.

She thrilled at the idea of having a dark, mysterious lover but knew she wasn't really unconventional enough to live outside the bounds of marriage. Her dilemma was that she wanted the best of both worlds. She wanted a dark, mysterious lover but wanted him to be her husband.

When they entered the casino an hour later, the first thing Zoe noticed as they moved among the glittering crowd was the abundance of different languages being spoken. English, Arabic, Italian, French, German. Some of the players were number crunchers with computerized systems for betting, while others were clearly risk takers who played with their gut instincts.

All were better gamblers than the two of them. They lost their gambling money in very short order and were happy to leave the rather stuffy casino to seek their thrills elsewhere.

They struck out on their second try as well.

The disco they chose asked thirty-five dollars a beer, and the young women in minidresses kept coming up and asking Grey to dance with them. He didn't have to ask her twice if she wanted to leave the disco. She

wanted their last night together to be special. She didn't
want to share him.

Driving around, they found a spot with a view of the
city. Parking, they sat for a while, quietly taking in the
beautiful view of the city that twinkled with a million
tiny white lights against an inky sky and *Le Grand Bleu*,
the Mediterranean.

It was telling that he lighted a cigarette.

"So," he asked, "have you made a decision?"

"I need time, Grey. I don't know what to do."

"What about your marriage?"

"It won't be easy going back to it, and it could never
be the way it was when I left."

"I see."

She could feel him distancing himself from her.

"Well, you're a big girl. You have to decide what is
best for you. But . . ."

She turned to him. "I don't just want a piece of a
man's heart. I want it all—or nothing."

"So you are a better gambler, then, than one might
have expected from your showing at the casino. Perhaps all you need is a run of good luck."

He got out of the car and came round to help her out.
She stood in his arms, her head on his shoulder, the
balmy air whispering around them.

"I could stay here forever," she told him and sighed.

"In Monte Carlo or in my arms, *chérie?*" he whispered.

"It's taken me so long to raise my self-esteem that I
don't want to risk losing my newfound confidence by

making the wrong decision," she said. "And yes, I've grown rather fond of your arms."

"They are useless when they aren't holding you in them," he said, his tone distraught.

"You'll never forget me, you know."

"I know. But this has been a dream. A wonderful, exquisite dream. It's not real life, Grey."

He put his fingers to her lips, silencing her.

"It can be real if we both want it to," he insisted. "I want you desperately, Zoe. I want to take care of you."

"No. I had a husband who took care of me. What I need . . . want is a man who takes care *with* me."

"I can be that man," he vowed, pulling her close. "I love you."

Later, in the suite, he made wild, uninhibited, passionate love. His lovemaking—not the sweet, gentle lovemaking of her husband. That was the point when he whispered, "Did your husband ever do this to you . . . ?"

She caught her breath and then he took it away completely.

THEY WERE SILENT on the drive from Monaco to Nice early the next morning. The loneliness of parting put a pall over their last hours together. A pall dispelled by the dazzling cheerfulness of the bright flower markets and gardens of Nice.

After making the arrangements for the car and her ride back to Paris, they decided to climb up to the clifftop park called Château that offered a magnificent view of the Riviera.

She wore her jean jacket and narrow, short black skirt, and he wore his jeans and bomber jacket. Though they were warmly dressed against the chill of early morning as they strolled arm in arm across the green expanse of grass, exploring old ruins, their hearts were cold from their impending separation.

When they climbed down from the park, they stopped at an open-air café and shared a *salade niçoise* because they were in Nice, and because it was something to do to avoid repeating the goodbyes they'd said late into the night.

"I guess we should go," Grey said, checking his watch, neither of them really able to do more than push the new potatoes and green beans around on their plates.

Zoe laid down her fork, nodding, her face sad.

"Do you want me to drop you at the train station?" he asked.

"No. I'll see you off. I've got time to make it back to the train station after you leave."

Once they'd arrived at Nice International, they strolled leisurely to the departure area. He turned to kiss her goodbye before he passed through the metal detector.

"You know where to find me," he said.

"I know."

"I love you," he said.

"I know."

"Are you going to kiss me? A proper mistress would, you know," he said, seeing the tears dampening the corners of her eyes, and wanting desperately to leave her smiling.

"*Allez...allez...*" an impatient Frenchman urged him through the metal detector.

"I've got to go," Grey said, kissing her quickly and grabbling his duffel, tossing it onto the conveyor.

As Grey walked through the metal detector, the alarm sounded, and Zoe turned back to look at him.

"What the hell?" Grey swore.

"Monsieur...you will please empty your pockets," the guard said firmly.

Grey got his wish and left Zoe smiling as he pulled a pair of handcuffs—and a scrap of white satin and lace—from the pockets of his bomber jacket.

"Mon Dieu!" the Frenchman said with sudden respect.

ZOE'S TRIP back to Paris on the bullet train was a quick and smooth ride...physically. Emotionally it was pure hell. The very air around her seemed full of...nostalgia and longing. She was oblivious to her fellow passengers, looking out the window as the gray and green and gold of the countryside passed by.

The orange-and-blue train had her back in Paris before she had absorbed the fact that Grey was gone.

The days and nights they'd shared were all she might have of him.

She had to make a choice, had to decide how she was going to live her life.

13

ZOE LET HERSELF into the loft. Weary from the trip and the emotional exhaustion of parting with Grey, she tossed her bags onto the floor near the door and sank onto the sofa with a weary sigh.

The empty loft echoed with loneliness without her friend there to share it. She missed Lauren-Claire's friendly chatter.

The flashing light on the answering machine caught her eye and she talked herself into dragging body and soul from the sofa to hit the Replay button, then went to get herself something to drink.

Perhaps Lauren-Claire had called and left a message, she thought, smiling when she saw the tubes of Lauren-Claire's red lipstick stored in the refrigerator.

She wondered if her friend had indeed lassoed herself a cowboy.

Reaching past the lipsticks for a soda, she heard the answering machine finish rewinding with a click.

"Hi, Zoe...it's me."

"Hi," Zoe said to the empty loft as Lauren-Claire's cheery voice warmed the space.

"My plane just landed here in Dallas and..."

Zoe carried her drink to the sofa and sank back into it, pulling off her jean jacket as she continued to listen.

"... you didn't lie. The cowboys grow on trees down here. *Mon Dieu!* Would you look at that! There goes one now. He's *très* gorgeous, like your mystery man. Later, *chérie*."

The machine beeped and Zoe smiled. Now she really had something to worry about—she and every cowboy in Texas—Lauren-Claire on the loose in the Lone Star State.

"Hi, Zoe ... miss me?"

Zoe nodded as her friend left another message.

"I forgot to ask yesterday when I called. How's your mystery man? Have you actually met him yet? Gosh, I miss all the good stuff. I bet you two are already married. He probably swept you right off your feet the minute I left town. Oh, speaking of marriage, remember the *très* gorgeous cowboy I saw at the airport when I was talking to you on the phone yesterday?

"Well, I sort of accidentally tripped, and he had to be gosh darn shucks ma'am real gentlemanly and help little 'ol me up. Zoe, he's got shoulders as wide as Texas and the deepest, most soulful gray eyes. I want to bear his children ... yes!"

Zoe chuckled, picturing the scene at the airport, complete with Lauren-Claire batting her dark, sexy eyes, all schoolgirl innocence and whispery French accent. The poor, defenseless, no doubt six-foot tall cowboy didn't stand Custer's chance at Little Big Horn.

"And guess what . . . we've got a date tonight. He's picking me up in a few minutes to take me to Fort Worth to some cowboy place called Billy Bob's. Oh and Zoe, I found the pink mohair sweater you snuck in my luggage. Thanks, I'm wearing . . . Oops, there's the door. Later, *chérie*." The machine clicked off.

Zoe yawned and stretched, putting her feet up.

"Zo-oe . . . where are you? I bet you're out with your mystery man, aren't you? Or is he there with you now— is that why you aren't picking up?" Lauren-Claire asked with a girlish giggle. "Remember, you're not allowed to have a man in the loft without me being there to chaperone. . . ." More giggles.

Zoe didn't know whether to laugh or cry.

"Did I remember to thank you last night when I called, for lending me your pink mohair sweater? Blade loved it. Oh, that's not his real name, of course. Everybody just calls him that 'cause he's real good with a knife, you know."

Zoe nearly choked on the ice cube she was sucking. It had taken her forever to find an ice tray when she'd moved into the loft, she remembered inanely as Lauren-Claire continued.

"Anyway, I learned how to do some cotton-picking dance, I think that's what they called it, at Billy Bob's last night. I must have been real good at it. I left pink fuzz all over Blade's shirt, and he's taking me to the rodeo tonight.

"I've got to go, need to find me a pair of second-skin jeans if I'm going to hope to compete with all these beautiful Texas girls with legs that go up to their armpits. Did I mention that Blade is darlin' precious, as they say here in Dallas, and that it will be a major deal when I steal him right out from under all these southern belles' noses? Later, sug-gar." End of message.

Zoe was happy someone was happy. Lauren-Claire really seemed to be enjoying Texas and Blade. She hoped Lauren-Claire hadn't picked up some weekend pretender. She should have warned her friend that everybody in Texas wore boots and cowboy hats. Oh, well, Lauren-Claire was having a good time, it wasn't as if she were planning on marrying this Blade person or anything, she decided, kicking off her black flats and wriggling her tired toes.

"*Bonjour, Zoe* . . . it's me again. How come you're never there when I call? You haven't run off with your mystery man, have you? Not that I'd blame you, him being such a major hunk 'an all. . . . Zoe, if you're there, please pick up the phone. No? Well, you'll never guess.

"You know how I told you last night Blade was taking me to the rodeo. Well, he did. But darling' precious forgot to tell me this one little ol' thing . . . he was *in* the rodeo! Imagine! He rides these big ol' mean bulls that I wouldn't get within two states of.

"He got first prize at it, too. And he gave it to me. Said I was the only prize he wanted to take home. I think I'm in love!"

Zoe sat up straight. Lauren-Claire had gained her full and complete attention. She couldn't wait for and yet dreaded the next words out of Zoe's mouth.

"So guess what? Blade's taking me home to the ranch tonight for dinner to meet his parents. If they like me, I might just have lassoed me my cowboy, Zoe. What should I wear? I remember you saying something about gingham.... You were kidding, weren't you? Listen, here's the phone number where I'm staying. Call me as soon as you get in."

Zoe grabbed her purse and rummaged for paper and pen, scribbling down the number Lauren-Claire recited.

"Talk to you later, y'all...." Lauren-Claire signed off with a giggle.

Zoe brought her arm up and squinted at her watch. It was way too late to call. She'd have to return Lauren-Claire's call in the morning.

"Zoe, did you call me last night after I left for the ranch with Blade?" Lauren-Claire asked, the messages on the tape continuing. "Everything went really great and it got so late that Blade's parents asked me to spend the night." There was another giggle, followed by, "Not bad for a third date, *non?*"

Zoe groaned. She didn't like the sound of where this was heading. She tried to figure out just how many days it had been since Lauren-Claire had met Blade. It wasn't comforting to realize she hadn't had to use up the fingers on one hand in her calculation.

"You were kidding me about wearing gingham, weren't you? I haven't seen anyone wearing it since I got here, so I wore my flirty blue-and-white crepe de chine dress with the handkerchief-point short skirt. It must have been okay, 'cause I got invited back.

"And Zoe, you ought to see the ranch. It's thirty minutes east of Dallas . . . not nearly far enough for me to spend enough time alone with Blade . . . but it's huge. Why, *mon père's* vineyards would only take up the north forty, as Blade calls it. Be sure and call me when you get back in, okay, so I can tell you all about it . . . and my darlin' precious Blade. Miss y'all."

Zoe wondered if Lauren-Claire had called her parents and if she had told them about Blade.

She didn't have to wonder long.

"Zoe, me again. I hung up before I remembered I wanted to tell you that if *mon père* or *ma mère* happen to call you to ask about me—don't tell them about Blade. We want to surprise them."

We . . . ? Zoe mouthed silently, grabbing her pillow from the sofa and squashing it over her face.

There was a beep, the sound of static on the tape and then a click.

Must have been a wrong number, she decided with a shrug. And then a disquieting thought struck. Had Lauren-Claire hung up, giving up on reaching her?

"Come on . . . talk to me," Zoe coaxed the answering machine, leaving the sofa to see if any messages remained to be played.

She heard Lauren-Claire's voice again before she made it to the machine. Backing up, she fell onto the sofa with a sigh of relief. Her hands moved to rub her sleepy eyes and she yawned. This was like being a parent and getting a postcard home from camp from your child that said, "Having fun ... don't worry about the snakebite. The swelling is going back down. I think." Zoe's hands measured the pillow and she squeezed it. As soon as she saw her friend again, she was going to wring her carefree little neck.

"Zoe ... Zoe. Come on, be there, Zoe. Oh, darn, where are you? How can we keep missing each other? You must have called when I was out with Blade last night. I want him real bad.... That's what I wanted to talk to you about. I think he's going to ask me to marry him tonight, Zoe. Call me, okay?"

"Are you crazy?" Zoe said to the empty room. "Why ... why your parents will be ... They'll kill you ... and me."

She rose from the sofa to go to the phone. It didn't matter what time of night it was, she had to talk some sense into Lauren-Claire. Marriage wasn't a lark. It was serious business. However hard as she'd tried, she hadn't been able to make hers work.

Before she was able to pick up the receiver, the last message on the answering machine began to play.

"Zoe! Pick up the phone, Zoe! It's me, Lauren-Claire. Quit, cut it out, Blade. Come on, she'll hear you."

Zoe did in fact hear kissing sounds.

"Bla-a-ade, will you behave.... Mmm..."

There were the sounds of a playful scuffle, giggles and the clunk of the phone being dropped to the floor before Lauren-Claire's voice could be heard again.

"He asked me, Zoe. Can you believe it?"

"And you said no or maybe or anything but yes...." Zoe coaxed aloud.

"I said yes! I'm going to marry Blade. Isn't it wonderful? *Zoe?* Blade, it's two in the morning in Paris, why isn't she at the loft? I hope nothing has happened to her. She'd call me if it had, wouldn't she, Blade?"

Zoe heard the sound of her friend's palm slapping her forehead. "What am I saying? What if she can't call? What if that mysterious guy who was following her kidnapped her or something? What if he was good-looking and dangerous? *Blade!*"

The tape ran out, clicked and began rewinding.

Zoe picked up the phone, then set it down and went to get the piece of paper on which she'd scribbled Lauren-Claire's number. She needed to reassure her friend and find out about this wedding business. Surely Lauren-Claire wasn't serious.

It had been less than a—well, it had been a week, but what could anyone find out about someone in a week? Her mind traveled over the week she'd spent with Grey as she waited for the call to go through. She'd learned things about him that she hadn't learned about her husband in the many years of their marriage.

So what was she going to tell Lauren-Claire? How could she advise her about anything, when she didn't know what she was going to do with her own life?

The call went through, saving her from trying to answer that question.

"Hello," Zoe said, telling the hotel clerk to ring Lauren-Claire's room.

After a few minutes the hotel clerk came back onto the line. "I'm sorry, ma'am, but she has already checked out of the hotel."

"*What?*"

"She has already checked out," the clerk repeated, audibly growing impatient.

"But that's not possible!" Where would she have gone? No, she didn't want to think about that. "Did she leave any messages?" she asked instead.

"One moment. I will check for you, ma'am." The hotel clerk laid down the phone and she could hear him waiting on someone else . . . the minutes of long distance expensively ticking away while he chatted. Finally he returned to the phone. "I've checked, ma'am, and there are no messages."

He hung up before she could say thank-you, not that she would have.

Now what? She rubbed her temples with her fingers. She was too tired to think. Whatever she decided to do, it would have to wait until the morning. She needed a good night's sleep.

A shower, she thought, and then to bed.

Picking up her bags, she began unpacking. Each item she pulled out was accompanied by a memory: the white cotton antique gown...black satin tap pants and demi bra ... pale pink hipster panties and matching cropped top... the white garter belt and white lace bra...she laughed upon seeing it. Grey or some French airport attendant had the matching white satin and lace thong bikini....

Emptying another bag, she came across the red leather *bustier* with gold studs, black taffeta evening pants and matching shoes ... the two-piece outfit Grey had bought her to wear to the beach.... Closing her eyes, she could still feel his hands on her, making her come all undone.

Shaking her head to clear it, she emptied the bag of its last contents, a handful of ribbons and a small box, containing the exquisite stickpin he'd bought her as a memento of their trip together. She fingered the piece of jewelry lovingly, then set it aside. Sniffling, she rose to go take her shower.

As the warm water rushed over her, she thought of Grey.

He'd probably forgotten all about her by now. For him the week had no doubt been nothing more than a salve to his ego. A macho thing.

When she turned off the shower, she heard the phone ringing. Grabbing a towel, she ran to catch it before Lauren-Claire missed her again.

She was too late.

And there was no message, just the click of someone hanging up.

Darn, she'd missed Lauren-Claire, and how was she ever going to locate her now? She'd just have to wait in the loft until her friend called back again.

STANDING AT A PAY PHONE in the middle of a frenetic New York airport, Grey hung up the receiver with a resigned sadness. Shouldering his duffel, he shoved his hands into the pockets of his bomber jacket and walked into the night . . . a lonely, romantic figure.

14

THE POUNDING on the door woke Zoe the following morning.

"I'm coming, I think..." she said, suffering from train lag or something as she tried to walk to the door of the loft and tie the sash on her robe at the same time.

She couldn't imagine who would be pounding on her door at such an ungodly—she picked up her watch and squinted at it. It was noon.

Finally making it to the door, she cracked it open, seeing a rather burly-looking young man with long hair.

"What is it?" she asked.

"Oh, you're American. Well, you're in luck. I speak English. I play in a rock band and only do this on the side," he said, indicating the clipboard in his hand. "Got a package for you *mademoiselle*."

"Leave it in the hall and I'll pick it up later."

"I don't think so."

"Why not?"

"Because it's going to take me and my partner here just to carry it in. If you'll sign here, I'll go help him bring it up and we can be out of here," he said, shoving the papers on the clipboard under her nose.

"What? I didn't order any...."

But the man was already off to help his partner bring up the thing she hadn't ordered. Maybe Lauren-Claire had ordered it. She looked down at the papers.

They were in French.

"Okay, where do you want it, *mademoiselle?*" the burly man said as he and his helper came up with a box as tall as she was and several feet square.

"I don't know," she said honestly.

"This is a good spot," he assured her as the two men maneuvered the awkward box to a place by the door.

"I don't know. Could you move it over . . . ?"

"Sorry, we don't do decorating, *mademoiselle*. Did you sign the papers?" he asked, taking them from her.

She nodded, having decided the spot with the big red X was where she was supposed to sign.

"*Adieu, mademoiselle,*" the delivery man said, ushering his helper out.

"What on earth?" Zoe wondered, left standing in front of a box as big as an armoire.

She didn't know how to begin to start opening it.

Maybe if she had a cup of tea. She was filling the kettle with water when the pounding on the door began again.

Aha, the delivery men had discovered their mistake and returned to take the monstrosity back with them. Thank heaven, she hadn't gone and tried to tackle opening it.

"I tried to tell you—"

Her words were effectively cut off by the sight that met her: Cowboy boots, scuffed and worn...long, long legs in jeans that were belted by a championship rodeo buckle that would choke a—ah, a horse . . . shoulders as wide as Texas and soulful gray eyes.

If there was any doubt, and there wasn't, this was Lauren-Claire's Blade. He stood there, cleaning his fingernails with the wickedest-looking knife this side of Fort Worth.

"Morning, ma'am," he said, his voice deep and growly. He tipped his cowboy hat. "I sure do hope you're Zoe, ma'am."

"Zoe! So you're all right, after all!" Lauren-Claire squealed, launching herself into Zoe's arms, letting go of the mail she'd been sorting as she trailed up the steps.

"I was so worried about you," Lauren-Claire said, breaking away from the hug.

"I can vouch for that. L.C. made me fly my daddy's private jet straight here."

"Zoe, this is my fiancé, Blade Wyatt. Isn't he just darling' precious, like I said? And would you look at the rock he gave me," Lauren-Claire said, lifting her hand to display an eight-karat solitaire diamond. "I swear I have to do finger exercises just to hold it up. I told him all I wanted was a little something romantic."

"Well, it is just a little something . . . a training ring. When we get married, I'll go to the jewelers and get you a real one. That one just came out of a gum-ball machine."

"Blade! Quit teasing!"

"Whatever you say, L.C."

Zoe smiled at the love glowing in Lauren-Claire's eyes when she looked up at her cowboy.

"And will you please—" Lauren-Claire shot Blade a look of reprimand "—put that wicked knife away and behave yourself. Zoe's from Texas, too, so you can't intimidate her with it. I swear, he's been having such fun flashing it all the way over here."

"Shucks," Blade mumbled, grinning and putting the knife into his boot.

"Zoe," Lauren-Claire asked as they went inside the loft, "why haven't you called me or been here when I called? And what is this?" she asked, running into the huge box that had been delivered only minutes earlier.

"You didn't order it?" Zoe asked.

"It?"

"I don't know what it is. The delivery receipt was in French, so I went ahead and signed it, thinking maybe you . . ."

"Why don't I just open it for you ladies, so you can find out what it is?" Blade offered.

"Thanks," Zoe said, relieved to have someone else handle the uncrating.

"You haven't explained about where you were," Lauren-Claire said as Blade went to work on the huge box, pulling out his knife to pry loose some nails.

Blade laughed, a deep rumble that was sexy and full of amused tolerance. "You'll have to excuse L.C. I get such a kick out of her cute little ol' French accent, I plum let her run roughshod and get her way 'bout most all the time. She's gotten kind of used to it this past week."

"Blade, will you quit? I'm serious."

"Me too, sugar. After the weddin' my momma is going to have to take you in hand and whip you into shape."

Zoe raised an eyebrow.

"Don't pay any attention to him," Lauren-Claire said, dismissing his comment with a wave of her hand. The splashy solitaire caught the light. "His momma drives a Jeep to her charity functions. Now are you going to tell me where you were or not?"

"No," Zoe answered, thinking Blade was perfect for Lauren-Claire.

"Good for you," Blade said, taking off the top of the crate. "Well, I'll be—look what we got us here!"

"What?" Lauren-Claire asked, coming over to the opened crate to have a look.

"I do believe it's a horsie," Blade answered with a chuckle as he lifted Lauren-Claire so she could see inside the crate.

"A what?" Zoe said, coming to have a look inside the crate, as well.

It was the carousel horse Grey had given her. She turned three shades of red, remembering the day. Grey wasn't playing fair at all.

"And here I thought you were just making an idle threat when you said you'd run away and join the circus, if I didn't accept your proposal of marriage," Blade said, laughing at Lauren-Claire.

"You hush, Blade. You're not supposed to tell anyone that I was the one who did the asking."

Blade turned to Zoe, his gray eyes full of laughter. "She begged me . . . real purty . . . on her knees."

"Blade Wyatt, will you hush!" Lauren-Claire said, hitting his arm.

"Ouch, you're hurting my tennis elbow, L.C.," he complained. Obviously a born storyteller, he continued blithely. "Funny thing is, I don't rightly remember saying yes."

By this time Zoe had forgotten her embarrassment and was laughing, as well.

"I just woke up the next morning with a smile on my face and absolutely no recall of why I'd thought it was such a dandy idea to remain a bachelor."

"Blade Wyatt, I do hope you don't think you're going to tell our children this yarn."

"Children . . . did I agree to *that*, too? Well, Momma will be proud. It must have been all that baby booze you plied me with."

"Baby booze?" Lauren-Claire and Zoe repeated.

"Yeah, that French champagne you kept insisting we toast each other with. . . . All those bubbles must have made me giddy." He then did a six-foot-four cowboy's rendition of feeling giddy and they were all on the floor, helpless with laughter.

When the laughter subsided, Zoe looked at Lauren-Claire and said, "I've really missed you. I'm glad you're back."

"Now don't be getting too used to having L.C. around. Just as soon as the weddin' comes off, I'm whisking her back to Texas and building her a house on the north forty."

"Suppose I don't want to live on the north forty," Lauren-Claire said, smiling sweetly.

"Well, then, I just guess you're going have to do some more of that begging you do so purty...."

"Blade!"

"Go on, L.C., Zoe's a Texas gal, there ain't no shocking them."

"When's the wedding?" Zoe asked, realizing suddenly that Lauren-Claire really would be gone again soon.

"In three weeks. We're going to announce our engagement to *mon père* and *ma mère* tonight."

"Why don't we elope and announce the wedding instead?" Blade suggested.

"Because, darlin' precious, my father would have y'all stomped to death in one of the wine vats."

"I think I can wait three weeks," Blade said on a falsetto note as he got up to finish uncrating the carousel horse.

"Now, are you going to tell me about this present and just what exactly has been going on since I've been gone, and whether or not it involves your *très* gorgeous mystery man?" Lauren-Claire demanded.

IT WAS QUIET in the loft when Lauren-Claire and Blade left to tell their news to her parents. Zoe smiled, thinking she'd like to be a mouse in the room when Blade walked in with their baby daughter.

Alone with her thoughts, Zoe stood running her hands over the exquisitely carved carousel horse Blade had placed by a window. It wasn't fair of Grey to have sent her this constant reminder of what they'd shared together.

In the next three weeks she was going to have to make up her mind about whether she was going to stay in Paris or return to the States.

And if she went back to the States, whom would she be going back to?

Could she bear to give up her dark, mysterious lover?

Could she *not* give her marriage another chance? Her husband *did* love her, and with that as a sound basis, they might be able to work out a marriage that fulfilled both their needs. He could, after all, provide her with the security she craved—and the excitement of the past week.

Couldn't he?

Or could one truly only be intimate with a stranger?

Could one have the erotic, unbelievably sexy lovemaking she and Grey had shared, when marriage and day-to-day living intruded with all of its demands?

Would her husband really be able to resolve their problems? Or would he continue to be seduced by his role as breadwinner, a role ingrained by generations of tradition?

She knew she would shrivel and die if she went back to living the kind of life she'd abandoned. Things *had* to change. She had.

One taste of Grey's passion, his uncontrolled imagination, and his sheer enjoyment of her had forever claimed her from a life of acceptance. She could no longer just exist. She had to act.

And her decision was going to have to be made in the midst of Lauren-Claire's whirlwind wedding plans.

She shook her head. Before she'd left with Blade, Lauren-Claire had insisted Zoe agree to be in the wedding.

How was she going to survive?

15

LAUREN-CLAIRE'S family estate of vineyards was located in the heart of champagne country, just ninety minutes outside Paris, close to a storybook village right out of once-upon-a-time.

The day of the wedding had dawned sunny and warm, dispelling the fears of the mother of the bride that her outdoor reception was going to be ruined by rain.

The wedding ceremony was being held in a private chapel located in the shelter of towering pines. Sunlight filtered in through the stained-glass windows, casting a rainbowlike hue upon the bride and groom. The reception afterward would be a much bigger social affair, but the chapel was small and held only the immediate family and a few friends.

Zoe waited for her cue in the back of the Gothic chapel as the two young flower girls tossed white rose petals to either side as they walked down the aisle.

The wedding was a merging of dynasties from two different worlds, as the assembled wedding guests made clear. On one side of the chapel were the groom's guests ... all three-hundred-dollar snakeskin cowboy boots with Western-cut suits, their ladies in chic designer outfits. On the other side was the bride's family...all expensive leather loafers and women in flower-strewn, feathered and beribboned hats with floaty dresses.

The music started and Zoe began to walk up the aisle, a fog of memories of her own wedding swirling around her. When she got to the front of the chapel, she blinked and saw Blade standing beside the waiting priest—towering over the priest, actually. Blade gave her a friendly wink as she took her place to the left of the priest.

They turned with the guests to watch the bride come down the aisle.

Lauren-Claire was a vision...a blending of the old and the new.

Despite a battle royal with her mother, she'd refused to wear her *grand-mère*'s wedding dress. Instead Lauren-Claire wore a perfectly cut, white designer silk pant suit. She'd compromised with her mother by agreeing to wear *Grand-mère*'s headpiece—a wide-brimmed white hat swathed in netting. The hat was the perfect fantasy complement to the sophisticated suit and set off Lauren-Claire's dark beauty.

For her wedding bouquet she carried several stems of white tulips.

The groom looked as though he was going to faint on the spot. He swallowed nervously as Lauren-Claire slipped her small hand into his large one and smiled up at him. Turning to face the priest, the exchange of vows began.

As Zoe listened to the same vows she'd exchanged with her husband, she fingered the antique stickpin she wore on the blush-pink suit Lauren-Claire had picked out for her. Tears formed in the corners of her eyes.

Then she heard the priest say, "You may kiss the bride," and Blade laid a Texas-sized kiss upon his new wife.

The music began again, and the wedding party filed out of the chapel into bright sunlight.

Lauren-Claire's mother fussed around her daughter, telling Blade's mother, "The child has a perfectly exquisite wedding dress from her *grand-mère* that she could have worn, but no, she had to wear pants.... *Mon Dieu!*"

Blade laughed. "That's because she thinks she's going to wear the pants in our marriage, but we're going to discuss that during the honeymoon tonight, aren't we, L.C.?"

"Blade!" Lauren-Claire said, punching his arm.

Blade's mother laughed. "Looks like we've raised a couple of spoiled children, perfect for each other, if they don't kill each other first."

"Dying on my honeymoon night, now wouldn't that be poetic?" Blade said, swooping Lauren-Claire into his arms for a kiss.

"Blade, put me down!"

"But don't I have to go carry you over a threshold?" he teased.

"That's the honeymoon, son," Blade's father—a dead ringer for John Wayne—informed him. "The reception comes first and as I recall it seems to go on forever."

"In that case, L.C., why don't we just skip the reception?"

"He's just like his father," Blade's mother said, shaking her head. "I've never been able to do a thing with either of them."

"There's food at the reception…barbecue, or so my wife tells me," Lauren-Claire's father suggested.

"Well, I guess we could stay for a few minutes. Barbecue, did you say?" Blade set Lauren-Claire down.

"Where are you going on your honeymoon?" one of Lauren-Claire's cousins piped up.

Lauren-Claire winked at Zoe. "There's this beach in Cannes I've heard good things about."

"Topless, I hope," Blade said, unrepentant, as the wedding party moved toward the tables of food.

While the meal was a Texas barbecue in honor of the groom, the desserts were very definitely French: *chocolat noir* cake, delicate apple tartlet, smooth coffee crème caramel and *millefeuille* with raspberry sauce.

Zoe nibbled the chocolate cake as she watched the happy couple with warring emotions; happiness and joy for her friend, a lonely sadness for herself.

There was, she noted, one Texas dessert. Pralines from a little chocolate shop in Paris called Au Duc de Praslin.

The groom was seen to pocket a few of them, just before he swept his bride off her feet and went off in search of thresholds to cross.

There were, Zoe thought to herself with a smile, yarns in the making.

L.C. had met her match . . . her perfect match.

BACK IN PARIS, Zoe went on with her life.

As a gift for being in the wedding, Lauren-Claire had given her the loft for a month with the rent paid. At the end of that time she would have to make a decision.

She continued to paint the tourists. But it wasn't the same without Lauren-Claire.

The loft was crowded, even though Lauren-Claire was gone. It was crowded, thanks to the presence of the carousel horse.

She couldn't escape its reminder. Wasn't sure if she wanted to.

And yet. There was a freedom in living in Paris without expectations. If she decided to leave, would she be giving up that freedom?

What did she want?

Did she want the handsome stranger who had taken her places she'd never been before?

Did she want the safety of marriage . . . the sweet gentleness of her husband?

Her hand was trailing over the carved head of the carousel horse when the phone rang.

It was Lauren-Claire, back in Texas from her honeymoon.

"How does it feel to be married?" Zoe asked.

"Oh Zoe, it's wonderful! And guess what . . . we're not living on the north forty. Blade's agreed to our living in Dallas and visiting the ranch on weekends."

"How did you convince him to agree to that?" Zoe asked, pretty sure of the answer.

"I got him at a weak moment," Lauren-Claire said on a giggle.

"A very weak moment," Zoe heard Blade call out in the background.

"How is Blade?"

"Oh, the doctor said without lots of bed rest specifically, he may live."

"Without lots of bed rest specifically, I may not want to live," Blade called out, loudly enough for Zoe to hear.

"Hush, Blade. Zoe and I want to talk. Have you decided what you want to do, Zoe? Are you going to stay on in Paris or return to the States?"

"I'm not sure yet," Zoe lied.

"Well, you can come stay with us anytime you want."

"Thanks, I appreciate your offer."

"You have to come to the christening, for sure."

"What?"

"I said . . ."

"I heard you.... Are you pregnant, Lauren-Claire?"

"Well it's a little soon to tell, but I hope so."

There was a scuffling sound and giggles, then Blade came onto the line. "L.C. has to go now, we have to make sure she's pregnant. Bye, y'all."

Zoe hung up the phone.

She knew what she had to do, had known it since Lauren-Claire and Blade's wedding.

She had to return to the States and give her marriage another try. She still loved her husband.

ZOE TRIED reading the magazines she'd brought with her. The best she'd been able to do was look at the fashion magazines. Pictures didn't take much concentration.

Since the plane had lifted off, she'd been a bundle of nerves.

Was she doing the right thing? Would she regret giving her marriage another try?

What would her husband think? Did he want *her* back?

Or did he just miss having a wife? Someone to be there for him when he needed her. Had he learned a wife had needs, too? Would he be willing to make the real changes necessary for their marriage to work? Or would he only slip back into his old habits.?

She knew she could never go back to how her marriage had been. She'd had a taste of living independently in Paris, and while it was sometimes lonely, freedom was exhilarating. Something she wasn't willing to give up.

She wanted a marriage of equals. She was no longer the little girl her husband had married, but a woman. A woman capable of finding satisfaction . . . and giving it.

The Fasten Your Seat Belts sign came on as the pilot announced the plane was about to land.

Putting the magazines into the rack in front of her, she fastened her seat belt and closed her eyes, praying for a safe landing.

HE STOOD at the terminal window, watching her plane land. He almost hadn't made it in time. The case he was working on had blown wide open at the last minute, and he'd had to commandeer a police car to get to the airport.

He couldn't believe she was returning—to him. He'd been so afraid he'd lost her.

When she'd made the reservation and his source had notified him, he'd almost wept with relief. Once she was on American soil, he had her. She'd never escape him again. After all, she was his wife. He'd make her love him again.

The plane landed and taxied down the runway to the terminal door where he waited.

Flashing his badge, he went ahead, before the plane could begin to empty. When he entered the cockpit, the pilot nodded, indicating that he'd been informed and made the announcement over the speaker system.

"Ladies and gentlemen, please remain in your seats. There is a policeman who has just boarded to take off his prisoner."

A mutter of interest swept through the passengers as they looked around to see who the prisoner might be.

"Nothing to be alarmed about folks, this is just a formality."

"Oh my God," Zoe said, sure her face had grown pale when she saw him heading down the aisle toward her, handcuffs dangling.

"Will you please come with me, ma'am?" he said, cuffing her, while the planeload of passengers looked on in amazement.

Her face was beet red as he grabbed her carry-on bag and led her from the plane, the badge he'd flashed the only thing identifying him as a cop in his jeans and bomber jacket.

"I'm going to kill you, Grey," Zoe said when they exited the ramp to the terminal.

"Now is that any way to talk to your husband?" he whispered into her ear, continuing to lead her handcuffed from the terminal, while the crowd gawked openly.

"You don't resemble the husband I left behind at all."

Grey chuckled. "I don't recall you complaining when I picked you up in that bistro in Paris. What made you go along with the fantasy that I was a stranger?"

"You were a stranger. The husband I left behind would never have thought of it. Why did *you* decide to play my fantasy lover?"

"I remembered all those romantic movies you rented when I was away so much. I decided to rent a few myself when you left and got a pretty good idea about what you were longing for in our marriage. I was listening when you voiced your unhappiness. I just didn't know what to do about it. Watching the movies you'd rented gave me the idea.

"I'd already discovered I had a darker side. Being a cop forced me to open my eyes to the world, a world that was more than my background. When I thought about it I realized you should be allowed to have more than one dimension to your personality too." His chuckle this time was very naughty. "Besides, I enjoyed the fantasy one hell of a lot."

"What were you thinking when you tried to pick me up in the bistro?"

"I was thinking that if you went along, life as we knew it would never be the same . . . *and I was glad.*"

"You know we can't go back to the way it was before I left."

"Are you kidding? I wouldn't think of it. And what were *you* thinking when I tried to pick you up in the bistro?"

It was Zoe's turn to laugh. "I was thinking . . . well, actually I wasn't thinking too well. You were so *hot* . . . it was exciting and scary and you know, Grey."

"Yeah."

"Can you take the cuffs off now?" she asked, trying to smile through gritted teeth when she noticed the crowd staring.

"I don't think so."

"Why not?"

"You owe me one, as I recall."

"Grey, if you don't take these cuffs off now, I'm going to scream!" she vowed.

"Why don't you keep that thought until we get home?" he said, looking at her with eyes that were hot with desire.

"You're not going to live that long. Grey, I'm warning you."

But he did live.

They both lived happily ever after.

IRRESISTIBLE NEW COVERS!

Over the past year we have been listening to our readers' comments and in response we have specially designed an attractive and eyecatching new cover for our Temptation series.

Available in the shops from August 1992 at the current price of £1.75.

This month's
irresistible novels from

─ TEMPTATIN ─

HOTLINE by Gina Wilkins

Assuming that the deep, melodious voice belonged to her brother, Erin Spencer talked on the phone quite happily... until she realized that the charming, witty man on the other end of the line was a total stranger!

FORBIDDEN FANTASY by Tiffany White

When Zoe fled her humdrum life to do everything she had dreamed of doing in Paris, she had never, even in her wildest thoughts, imagined a man like Grey. He was her every forbidden fantasy *and* he wanted *her*...

A LEGAL AFFAIR by Bobby Hutchinson

Zach Jones had ulterior motives for volunteering at the legal clinic. It was a great way to meet *impressionable* female students. He hadn't counted on being knocked out by red-haired Jenny Lathrop, however.

AN IMPERFECT HERO by Jo Morrison

Young and in love, Susan and Hank had married, ignoring all the warning comments, believing their passion for each other was enough. But was Hank's greatest fear coming true? Just how much did Sue need – or desire – him now?

Spoil yourself next month
with these four novels from

—TEMPTATI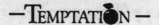N —

A DANGEROUS GAME by Candace Schuler

Natalie Bishop was a first-rate private investigator and when her brother's partner had a fatal accident she went into action. The prime suspect was the victim's own brother—Lucas Sinclair—and he was certainly guilty of being as sexy as sin.

DADDY, DARLING by Glenda Sanders

Dory Karol and Scott Rowland were perfectly happy with their long-distance affair, but then the unforeseen happened and Dory found herself pregnant. Marriage was not on Scott's agenda, so how was he going to react to the knowledge that he was about to become a daddy?

RIPE FOR THE PICKING by Mary Tate Engels

Annie Clayton enjoyed Brett Meyer's company, but she was a woman with something to hide, something that could put her on the other side of the law. It was inevitable that Brett would discover her secret. But did that mean that one day he would come to her as a lawman and not as her lover?

IT HAPPENED ONE WEEKEND by Vicki Lewis Thompson

Nowhere in Adrienne Burnham's appointment book was there room for rugged, devil-may-care Matt Kirkland! *He* lived for adventure and spontaneity. *She* liked life ordered and peaceful. She never should have accepted his offer to fly her home. . .

TEMPTATION

FORBIDDEN FANTASY
— *By Tiffany White* —

*We hope you have enjoyed reading
FORBIDDEN FANTASY by Tiffany White.*

**Regular readers will know that from time to time
we invite your opinion on our latest books, so that
we can be sure to continue to provide what you
want - the very best in romantic fiction.**

Please spare a few moments to answer the questions below
and we will send you an exciting FREE book as our thank you.

Please tick the appropriate box for each question ✓

1 Did you enjoy FORBIDDEN FANTASY?

Very Much ☐ Quite a Lot ☐ Not Very Much ☐ Not at All ☐

2 What did you like best about it?

The Plot ☐ The Hero ☐ The Heroine ☐ The Background ☐

3 What did you like least about it?

The Plot ☐ The Hero ☐ The Heroine ☐ The Background ☐

4 Did you find FORBIDDEN FANTASY contained:

Too Much Sex ☐ The Right Amount of Sex ☐ Too Little Sex ☐

5 Do you have any comments to make about FORBIDDEN FANTASY?

_____

_____

_____

6 What are your feelings about unfaithfulness between a husband and wife being included in Temptation books? _____

_____

7 How often do you read Temptation books?

Every Month ☐   Every 2 or 3 Months ☐   Less Often ☐

8 Which of the following series do you read?   •

Mills & Boon: Romance ☐	**Silhouette:** Sensation ☐	
Best Seller ☐	Special Edition ☐	
Medical Romance ☐	Desire ☐	
Collection/Duet ☐	**Loveswept** ☐	
Masquerade ☐	**Zebra** ☐	

9 Where did you get FORBIDDEN FANTASY from?

Mills & Boon Reader Service ☐   New from the Shops ☐

Other (please specify): _____

10 What age group are you?

16-24 ☐   25-34 ☐   35-44 ☐   45-54 ☐   55-64 ☐   65+ ☐

11 Are you a Reader Service subscriber?   Yes ☐   No ☐

If Yes, your subscription number is: _____

THANK YOU FOR YOUR HELP Please send to: Mills & Boon Reader Service, FREEPOST, P.O. Box 236, Croydon, Surrey, CR9 9EL.

FREEPOST - NO STAMP NEEDED

Please fill in your name and address to receive your FREE book:

Ms/Miss/Mrs/Mr _____ EDF

Address _____

_____ Post Code _____

mps MAILING PREFERENCE SERVICE